Ghost Stories
of an Antiquary

II

A Graphic Collection of Short Stories by M.R. James
Adapted by Leah Moore and John Reppion

SELF MADE HERO

First published in the UK 2017
by SelfMadeHero
139-141 Pancras Road
London NW1 1UN
www.selfmadehero.com

Publishing Director: Emma Hayley
Sales & Marketing Manager: Sam Humphrey
Editorial & Production Manager: Guillaume Rater
UK Publicist: Paul Smith
US Publicist: Maya Bradford
Designer: Txabi Jones
Editor: Dan Lockwood
Cover by: Francesco Francavilla

A CIP record for this book is available from the British Library

ISBN: 978-1-910593-39-4

10 9 8 7 6 5 4 3 2 1

Printed and bound in Slovenia

SOMETHING IS COMING

Almost one whole century before Japanese horror movie franchises like **Ring** and **The Grudge** popularised the concept of hideous supernatural beings stalking the hell out of us, M.R. James had already cornered the market in unstoppable dread. One of the most powerful aspects of his wonderful stories tends to be the sense that *something is coming*. Oh yes indeed, something is coming and there's absolutely nothing you can do to halt that thing's progress. Through curiosity, greed, vanity, stupidity, academic hunger or some combination of the above, you are royally screwed.

"Oh, Whistle, And I'll Come To You, My Lad" strikes me as the ultimate example of the Jamesian something-coming trope. I first encountered this story – and James himself – courtesy of Jonathan Miller's excellent 1968 TV adaptation, retitled **Whistle and I'll Come To You**. No matter which version you experience, there's something beautifully horrendous about a man dashing across a windswept beach, clambering desperately over groynes as he's pursued by some grimly flapping phantom. That's part of what horror is all about: transforming a traditional symbol of leisure and relaxation, such as the beach, into something to lose sleep over.

How great to see this immortal tale resurface in a new medium, thanks to Leah Moore, John Reppion and illustrator Al Davison. One of the adaptation skills displayed so consistently by the Moore-Reppion axis is the way they lightly boil down James' original prose, which so often features undeniably entertaining tangents and bewitching layers of detail. Their sure eye guarantees that the most memorable turns of phrase and key slivers of dialogue are all spared the chop. Furthermore, they shun the potentially easier route of entirely stripping James' work of its anecdotal, second-hand qualities. The pair could, for instance, have chosen to let Professor Parkins tell his story directly to the reader. But as we all know, James delivered his accounts of the follies of third parties as if passing on unearthly gossip in front of a crackling fire, armed with a stiff cognac. Besides creating a richly potent atmosphere, this clever approach added a whole other layer of eerie verisimilitude to the proceedings. Indeed, it's very hard not to think of M.R. James as having been the original pioneer of the contemporary artform known as creepypasta. He never even needed the internet.

A side note here: I don't know about you, but I usually can't help but derive no small measure of sadistic glee as I wait to see James' protagonists get the bejaysus scared out of them, often so badly that their cravats fall clean off. This is because they tend to be such pompous prigs, so very sure of themselves and therefore headed for a fall. So one pleasing advantage of the graphic novel medium is that we get to see their actual faces. I'm delighted to report that Professor Parkins' face, as drawn by Davison, is every bit as slappable as Dennistoun's was in Volume 1's "Canon Alberic's Scrapbook". Good times.

Having focused on "Whistle" for three whole paragraphs now, I wouldn't want to give the impression that the other three stories here are slouches. On the contrary, every one's a winner.

"Number 13" has always been a fun story in prose, being the tale of a man who questions why there's no Room 13 in his Viborg hotel... or is there? This one really lends itself to a visual rendering. While James did a bang-up job of painting the picture of a hotel with certain fluid properties, it was perhaps a tall order for the reader to visualise with absolute clarity. The ability to actually *see* all those shadows and window formations, courtesy of George Kambadais' splendid art, really helps to convey these concepts to your unnerved and quivering brain.

Equally, it is glorious to finally behold Abbot Thomas' cryptic stained glass window with your eyes, as opposed to your mind's eye, at the outset of "The Treasure of Abbot Thomas". The gorgeous colours of Meghan Hetrick's work here may intuitively seem at odds with a dark and scary tale, but this is not the case. Some things only become more frightening when you drag them into the light, and contrast can be a powerful weapon. One especially lovely panel shows Somerton and his long-suffering lackey Brown descending into the well, as if we are seeing straight through its walls. A real treat. It's worth mentioning, too, that a clear decision appears to have been made in this series to, more often than not, *show* readers the ghouls and ghosts, which I applaud. It's interesting to behold the writers' and artists' own interpretation of each foul fiend, and the reader is always at liberty to cling on to the original manifestation in their head.

As the mighty Ramsey Campbell noted in his Volume 1 foreword, James himself commissioned a handful of "Count Magnus" illustrations back in the day. All the more momentous, then, to see this creepy and **Blair Witch**-prefiguring story act itself out fully on the page, as etched by Abigail Larson. We finally get to witness the Count himself, his mysteriously insecure sarcophagus and, of course, what a certain character looks like without a face. When James does actually kill his characters, as opposed to merely scaring them into a stupor, he doesn't mess about. And once again, here's that Moore-Reppion knack for identifying essential lines: "Then they hear someone scream, just as if the most inside part of his soul was twisted out!"

It's a rare combination of words that makes you recoil from them, and James' work is awash with such extra-special stuff. He is undoubtedly one of the very finest purveyors of ghost stories ever to darken our doors. And Moore and Reppion have done the great man proud. If ghosts really do exist, then none will come for this dastardly duo on James' behalf, unless it's to offer them each a celestial cigar.

Jason Arnopp
Brighton, July 2017

CONTENTS

All stories adapted by Leah Moore and John Reppion

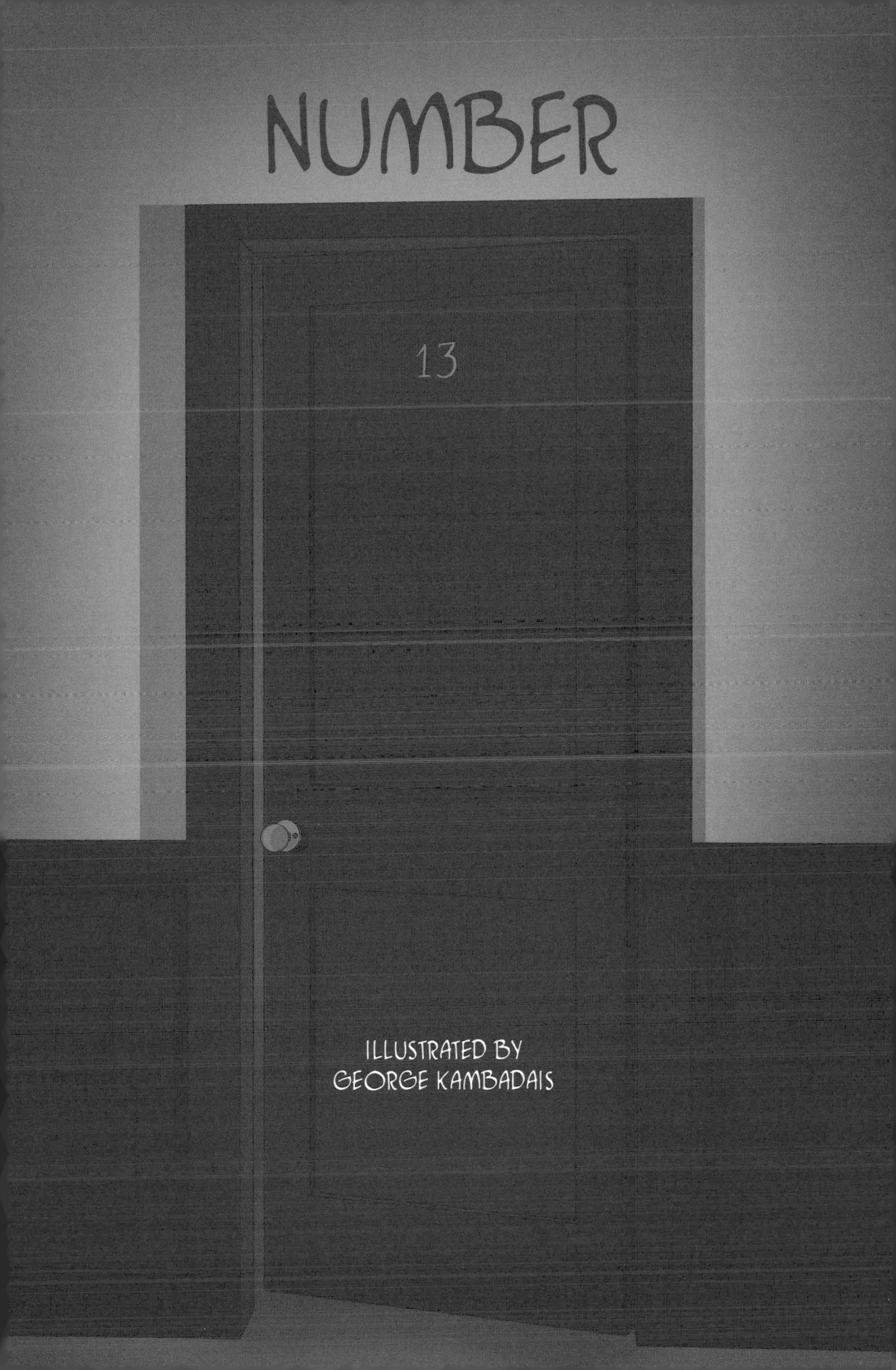
NUMBER
13
ILLUSTRATED BY
GEORGE KAMBADAIS

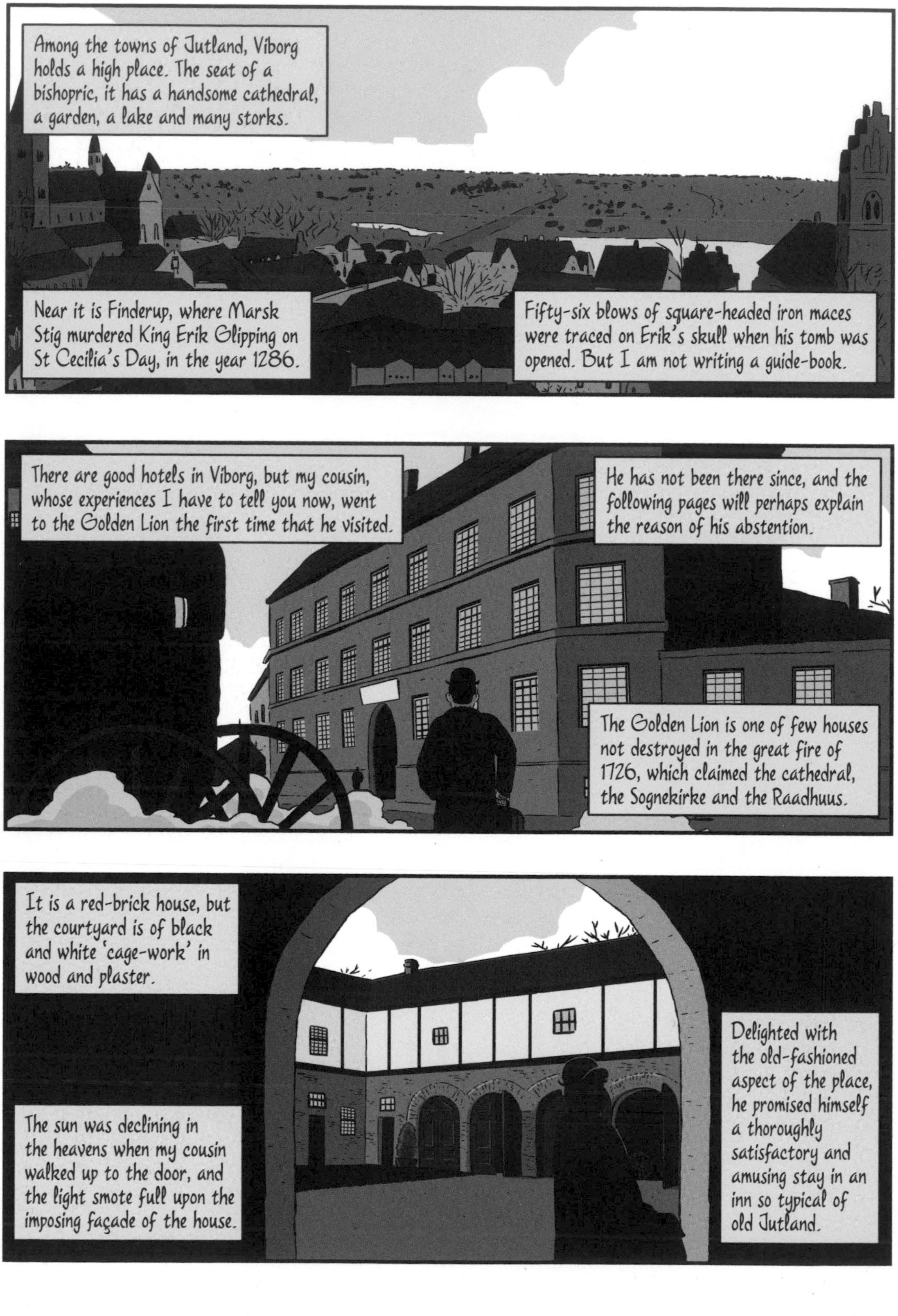
Among the towns of Jutland, Viborg holds a high place. The seat of a bishopric, it has a handsome cathedral, a garden, a lake and many storks.
Near it is Finderup, where Marsk Stig murdered King Erik Glipping on St Cecilia's Day, in the year 1286.
Fifty-six blows of square-headed iron maces were traced on Erik's skull when his tomb was opened. But I am not writing a guide-book.
There are good hotels in Viborg, but my cousin, whose experiences I have to tell you now, went to the Golden Lion the first time that he visited.
He has not been there since, and the following pages will perhaps explain the reason of his abstention.
The Golden Lion is one of few houses not destroyed in the great fire of 1726, which claimed the cathedral, the Sognekirke and the Raadhuus.
It is a red-brick house, but the courtyard is of black and white 'cage-work' in wood and plaster.
The sun was declining in the heavens when my cousin walked up to the door, and the light smote full upon the imposing façade of the house.
Delighted with the old-fashioned aspect of the place, he promised himself a thoroughly satisfactory and amusing stay in an inn so typical of old Jutland.

Mr Anderson was researching the Church history of Denmark.

The Rigsarkiv of Viborg contained papers, saved from the fire, relating to the last days of Roman Catholicism in the country.

He proposed to spend as much as a fortnight or three weeks examining and copying them.

Accordingly, he requested a room large enough to serve as both bedroom and study.

The landlord suggested he might pick the room himself.

The top floor was soon rejected as entailing too much getting upstairs after the day's work.

The second floor contained no room of exactly the dimensions required.

On the first floor, there were two or three rooms which would suit admirably.

The landlord suggested Number 17, but Anderson thought it would be very dark in the afternoon.

Eventually Number 12 was selected. Like its neighbours, it had three windows, all on one side of the room.

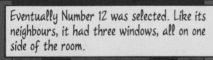

It was fairly high and unusually long.

It also looked out onto the street, and the bright evening light and the pretty view would compensate for any additional amount of noise.

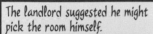

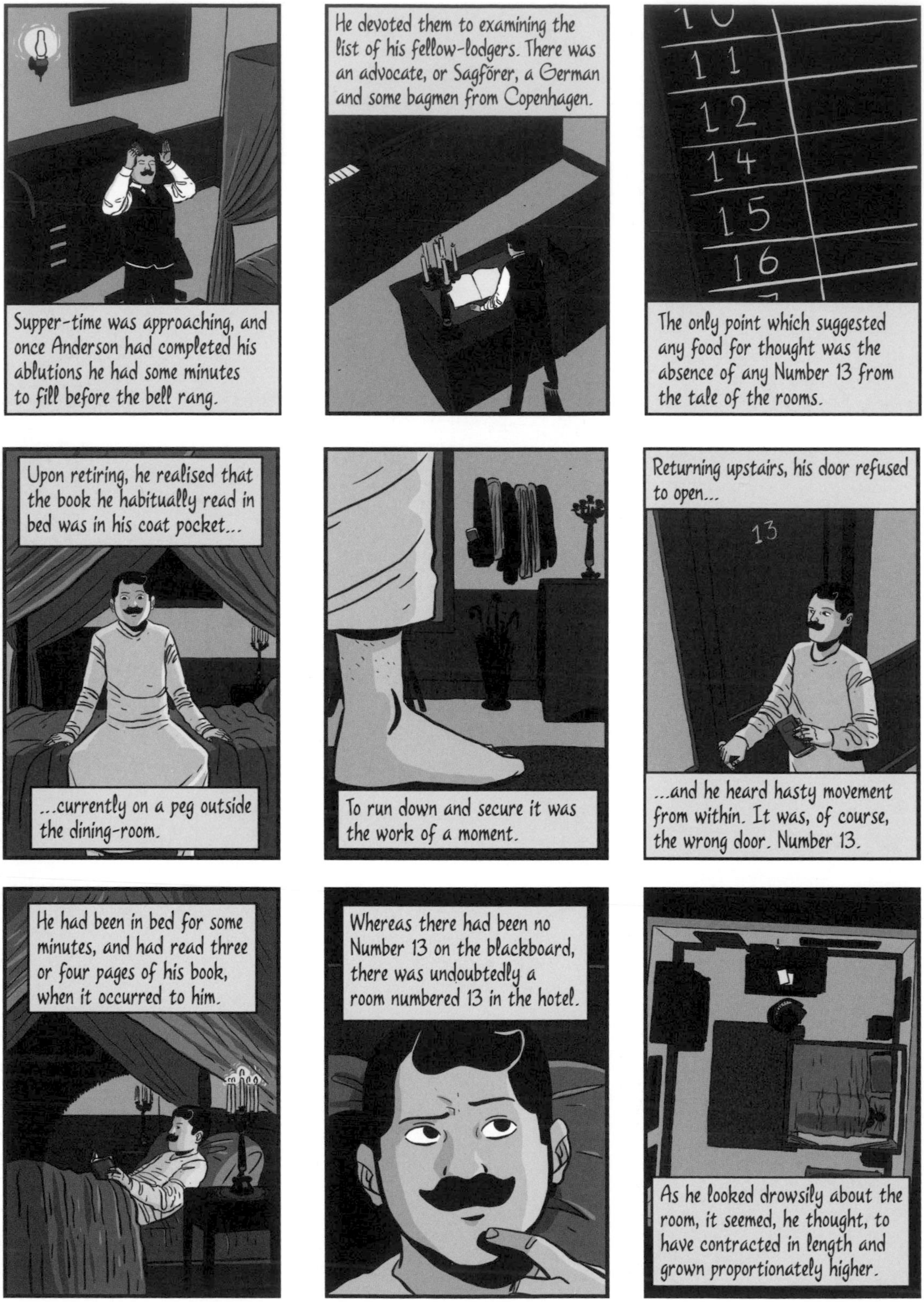
Supper-time was approaching, and once Anderson had completed his ablutions he had some minutes to fill before the bell rang.
He devoted them to examining the list of his fellow-lodgers. There was an advocate, or Sagförer, a German and some bagmen from Copenhagen.
11
12
14
15
16
The only point which suggested any food for thought was the absence of any Number 13 from the tale of the rooms.
Upon retiring, he realised that the book he habitually read in bed was in his coat pocket...
...currently on a peg outside the dining-room.
To run down and secure it was the work of a moment.
Returning upstairs, his door refused to open...
13
...and he heard hasty movement from within. It was, of course, the wrong door. Number 13.
He had been in bed for some minutes, and had read three or four pages of his book, when it occurred to him.
Whereas there had been no Number 13 on the blackboard, there was undoubtedly a room numbered 13 in the hotel.
As he looked drowsily about the room, it seemed, he thought, to have contracted in length and grown proportionately higher.

On the day after his arrival, Anderson attacked the Rigsarkiv of Viborg.

The documents were more numerous and interesting than he had anticipated. Besides official papers, there was a large bundle of correspondence.

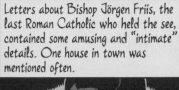

Letters about Bishop Jörgen Friis, the last Roman Catholic who held the see, contained some amusing and "intimate" details. One house in town was mentioned often.

In one such document, the writer complains that the tenant of the house "practised secret and wicked arts".

"It is typical of the gross corruption of the Babylonish Church that the bloodsucking *Troldmand Mag. Nicolas Francken* be harboured by Friis."

Friis insisted that his antagonists bring the matter before the spiritual court and "sift it to the bottom". Protestant leader Rasmus Nielsen replied that a Roman Bishop's Court was not a "competent tribunal".

Herr Scavenius, the Archivist of Viborg, though very well informed, was not a specialist in the Reformation period.

He was much interested in Anderson's findings.

"This house of the Bishop Friis is a mystery," Scavenius said.

"I studied the records of the Bishop's property, but the piece which had the list of the town property is missing."

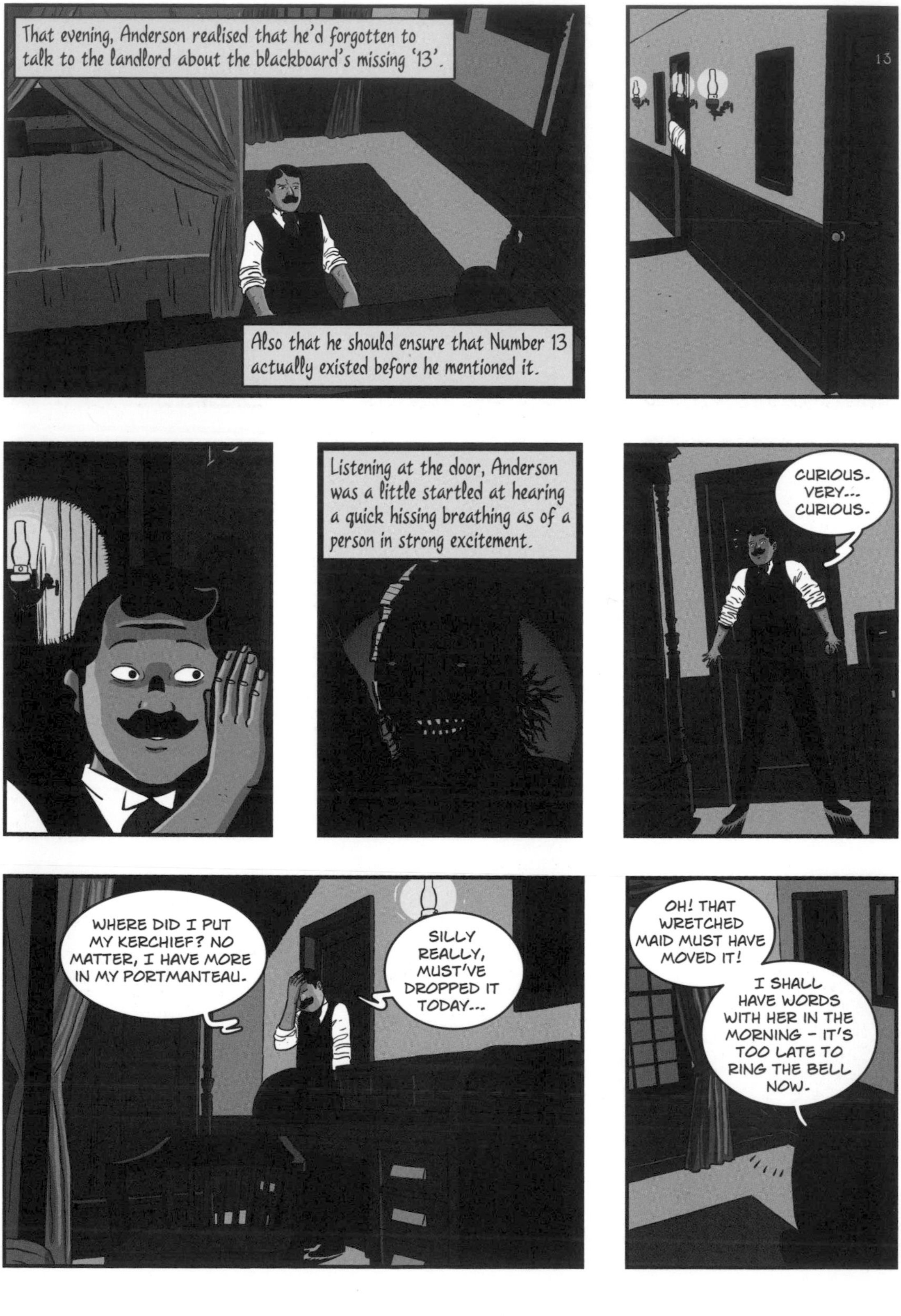

That evening, Anderson realised that he'd forgotten to talk to the landlord about the blackboard's missing '13'.
Also that he should ensure that Number 13 actually existed before he mentioned it.
13
Listening at the door, Anderson was a little startled at hearing a quick hissing breathing as of a person in strong excitement.
CURIOUS. VERY... CURIOUS.
WHERE DID I PUT MY KERCHIEF? NO MATTER, I HAVE MORE IN MY PORTMANTEAU.
SILLY REALLY, MUST'VE DROPPED IT TODAY...
OH! THAT WRETCHED MAID MUST HAVE MOVED IT!
I SHALL HAVE WORDS WITH HER IN THE MORNING - IT'S TOO LATE TO RING THE BELL NOW.

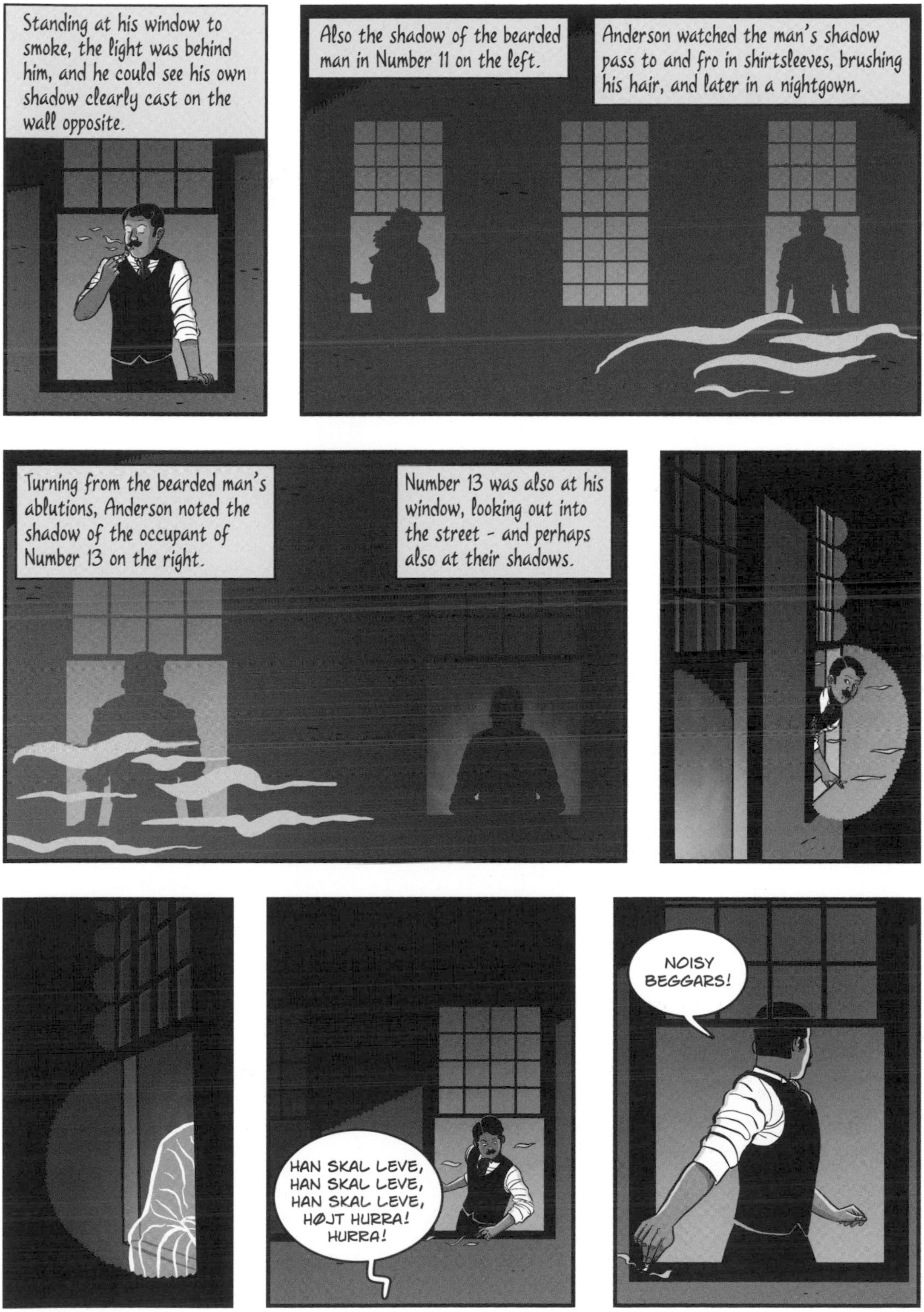
Standing at his window to smoke, the light was behind him, and he could see his own shadow clearly cast on the wall opposite.
Also the shadow of the bearded man in Number 11 on the left.
Anderson watched the man's shadow pass to and fro in shirtsleeves, brushing his hair, and later in a nightgown.
Turning from the bearded man's ablutions, Anderson noted the shadow of the occupant of Number 13 on the right.
Number 13 was also at his window, looking out into the street - and perhaps also at their shadows.
HAN SKAL LEVE, HAN SKAL LEVE, HAN SKAL LEVE, HØJT HURRA! HURRA!
NOISY BEGGARS!

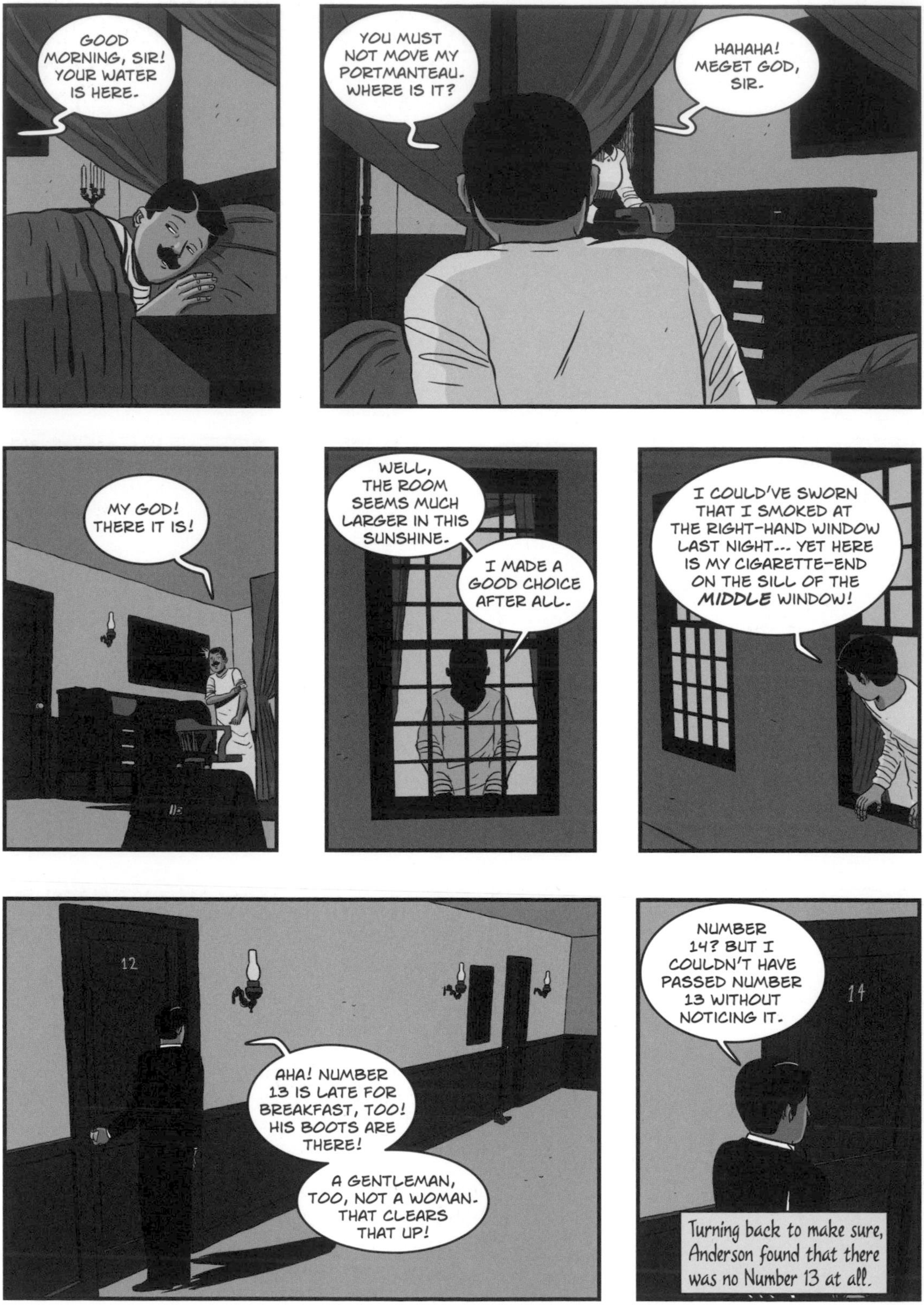
GOOD MORNING, SIR! YOUR WATER IS HERE.
YOU MUST NOT MOVE MY PORTMANTEAU. WHERE IS IT?
HAHAHA! MEGET GOD, SIR.
MY GOD! THERE IT IS!
WELL, THE ROOM SEEMS MUCH LARGER IN THIS SUNSHINE.
I MADE A GOOD CHOICE AFTER ALL.
I COULD'VE SWORN THAT I SMOKED AT THE RIGHT-HAND WINDOW LAST NIGHT... YET HERE IS MY CIGARETTE-END ON THE SILL OF THE MIDDLE WINDOW!
12
AHA! NUMBER 13 IS LATE FOR BREAKFAST, TOO! HIS BOOTS ARE THERE!
A GENTLEMAN, TOO, NOT A WOMAN. THAT CLEARS THAT UP!
NUMBER 14? BUT I COULDN'T HAVE PASSED NUMBER 13 WITHOUT NOTICING IT.
14
Turning back to make sure, Anderson found that there was no Number 13 at all.

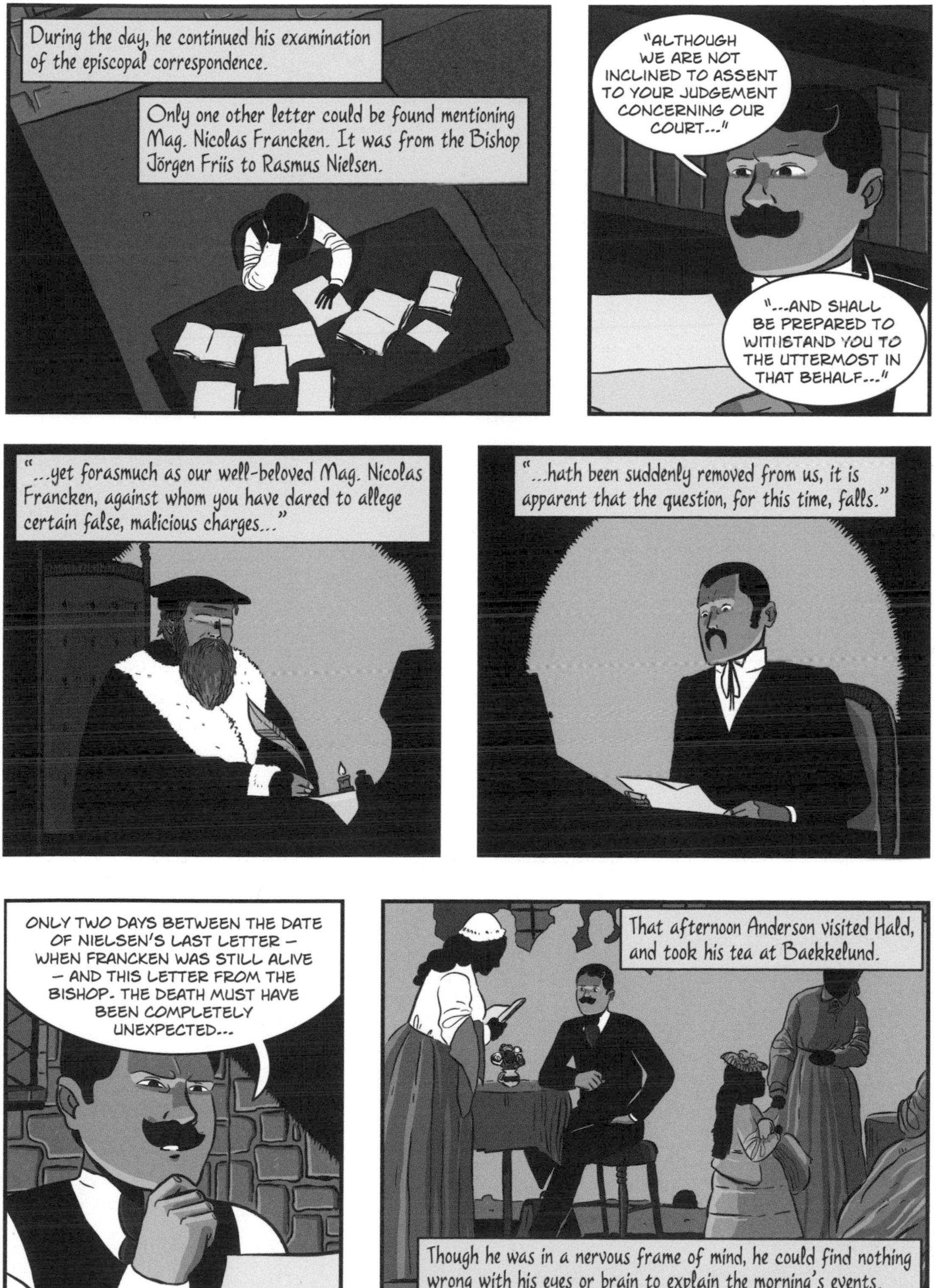
During the day, he continued his examination of the episcopal correspondence.
Only one other letter could be found mentioning Mag. Nicolas Francken. It was from the Bishop Jörgen Friis to Rasmus Nielsen.
"ALTHOUGH WE ARE NOT INCLINED TO ASSENT TO YOUR JUDGEMENT CONCERNING OUR COURT..."
"...AND SHALL BE PREPARED TO WITHSTAND YOU TO THE UTTERMOST IN THAT BEHALF..."
"...yet forasmuch as our well-beloved Mag. Nicolas Francken, against whom you have dared to allege certain false, malicious charges..."
"...hath been suddenly removed from us, it is apparent that the question, for this time, falls."
ONLY TWO DAYS BETWEEN THE DATE OF NIELSEN'S LAST LETTER – WHEN FRANCKEN WAS STILL ALIVE – AND THIS LETTER FROM THE BISHOP. THE DEATH MUST HAVE BEEN COMPLETELY UNEXPECTED...
That afternoon Anderson visited Hald, and took his tea at Baekkelund.
Though he was in a nervous frame of mind, he could find nothing wrong with his eyes or brain to explain the morning's events.

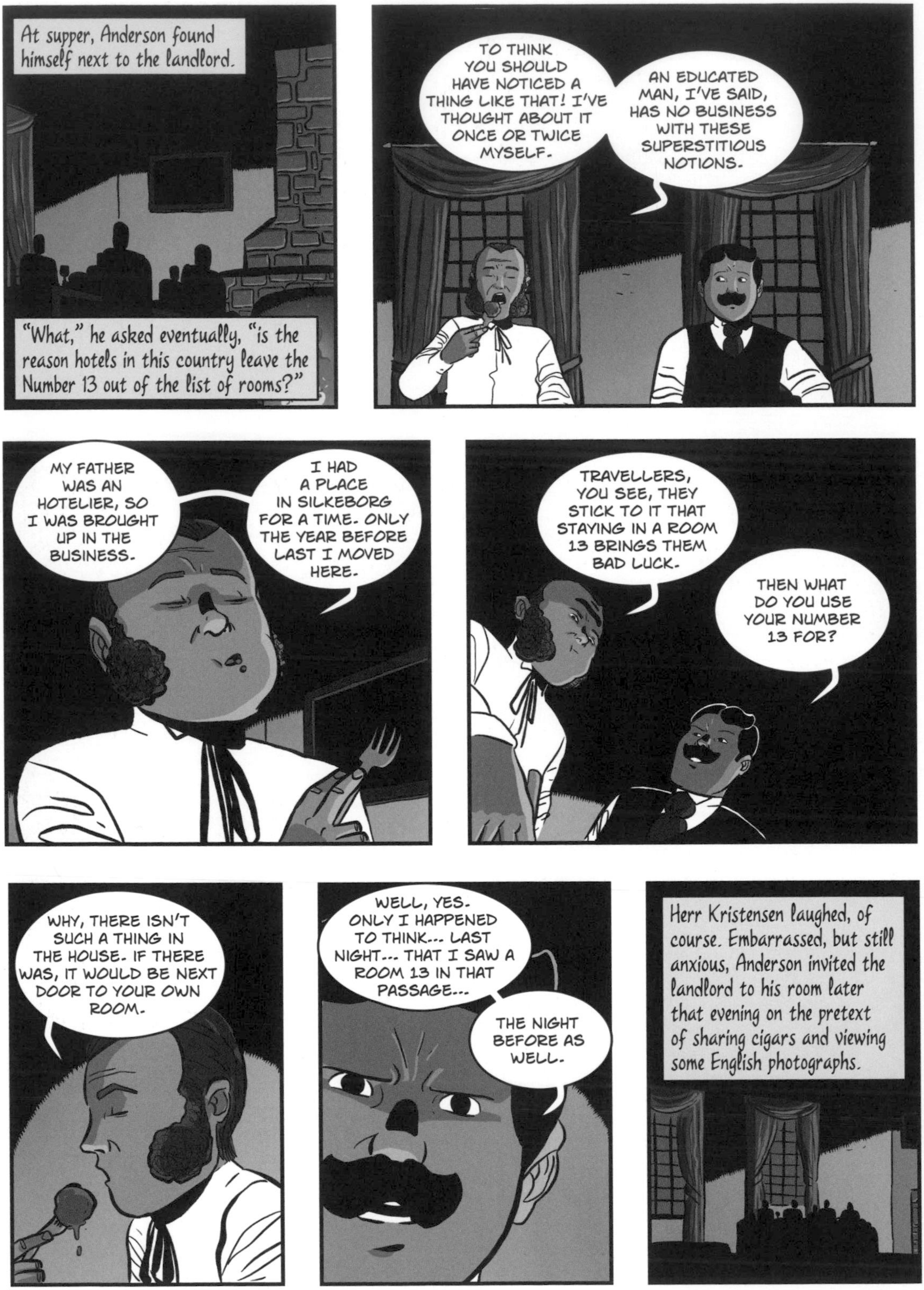
At supper, Anderson found himself next to the landlord.
"What," he asked eventually, "is the reason hotels in this country leave the Number 13 out of the list of rooms?"
TO THINK YOU SHOULD HAVE NOTICED A THING LIKE THAT! I'VE THOUGHT ABOUT IT ONCE OR TWICE MYSELF.
AN EDUCATED MAN, I'VE SAID, HAS NO BUSINESS WITH THESE SUPERSTITIOUS NOTIONS.
MY FATHER WAS AN HOTELIER, SO I WAS BROUGHT UP IN THE BUSINESS.
I HAD A PLACE IN SILKEBORG FOR A TIME. ONLY THE YEAR BEFORE LAST I MOVED HERE.
TRAVELLERS, YOU SEE, THEY STICK TO IT THAT STAYING IN A ROOM 13 BRINGS THEM BAD LUCK.
THEN WHAT DO YOU USE YOUR NUMBER 13 FOR?
WHY, THERE ISN'T SUCH A THING IN THE HOUSE. IF THERE WAS, IT WOULD BE NEXT DOOR TO YOUR OWN ROOM.
WELL, YES. ONLY I HAPPENED TO THINK... LAST NIGHT... THAT I SAW A ROOM 13 IN THAT PASSAGE...
THE NIGHT BEFORE AS WELL.
Herr Kristensen laughed, of course. Embarrassed, but still anxious, Anderson invited the landlord to his room later that evening on the pretext of sharing cigars and viewing some English photographs.

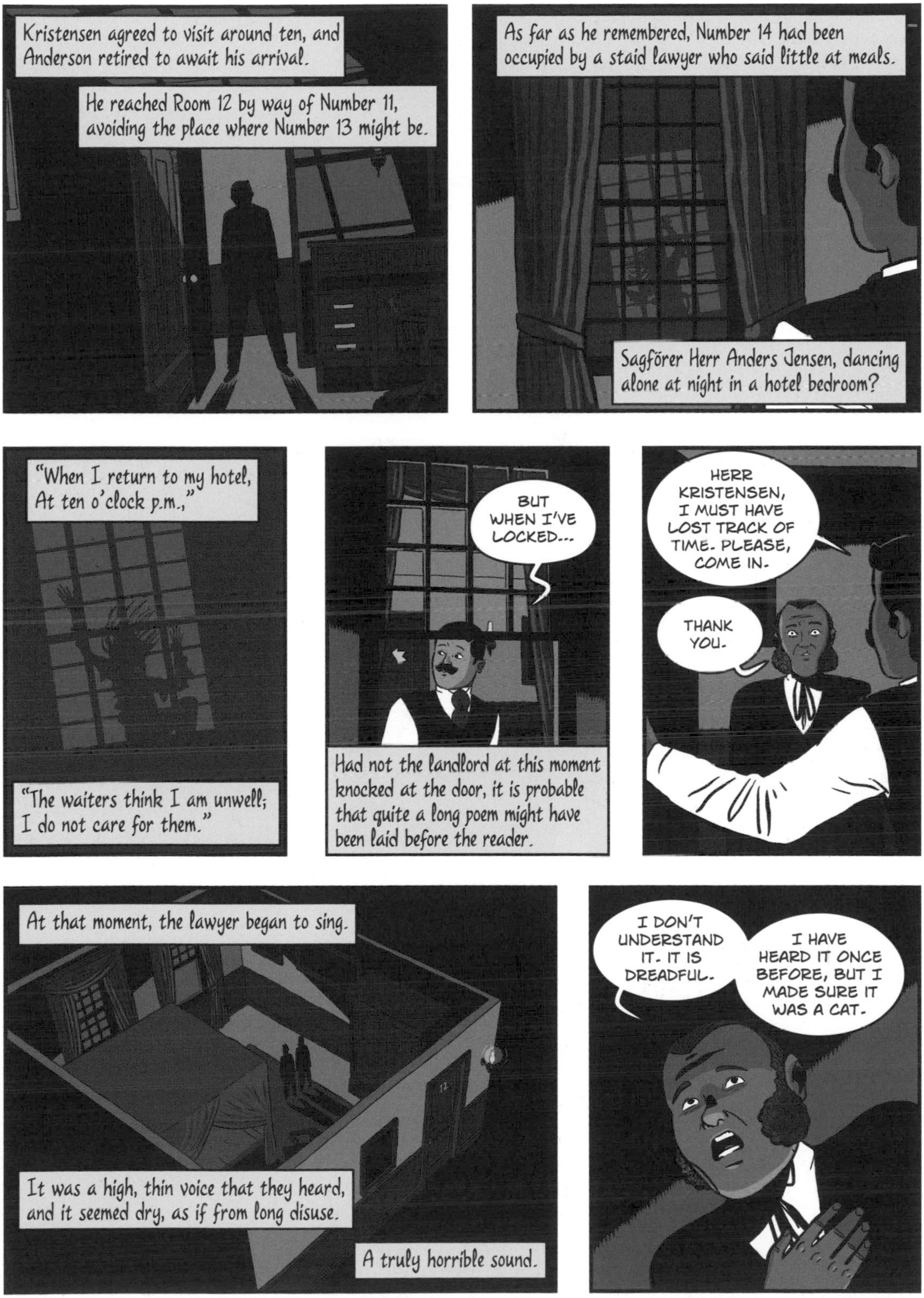
Kristensen agreed to visit around ten, and Anderson retired to await his arrival.
He reached Room 12 by way of Number 11, avoiding the place where Number 13 might be.
As far as he remembered, Number 14 had been occupied by a staid lawyer who said little at meals.
Sagförer Herr Anders Jensen, dancing alone at night in a hotel bedroom?
"When I return to my hotel, At ten o'clock p.m.,"
"The waiters think I am unwell; I do not care for them."
BUT WHEN I'VE LOCKED...
Had not the landlord at this moment knocked at the door, it is probable that quite a long poem might have been laid before the reader.
HERR KRISTENSEN, I MUST HAVE LOST TRACK OF TIME. PLEASE, COME IN.
THANK YOU.
At that moment, the lawyer began to sing.
12
It was a high, thin voice that they heard, and it seemed dry, as if from long disuse.
A truly horrible sound.
I DON'T UNDERSTAND IT. IT IS DREADFUL.
I HAVE HEARD IT ONCE BEFORE, BUT I MADE SURE IT WAS A CAT.

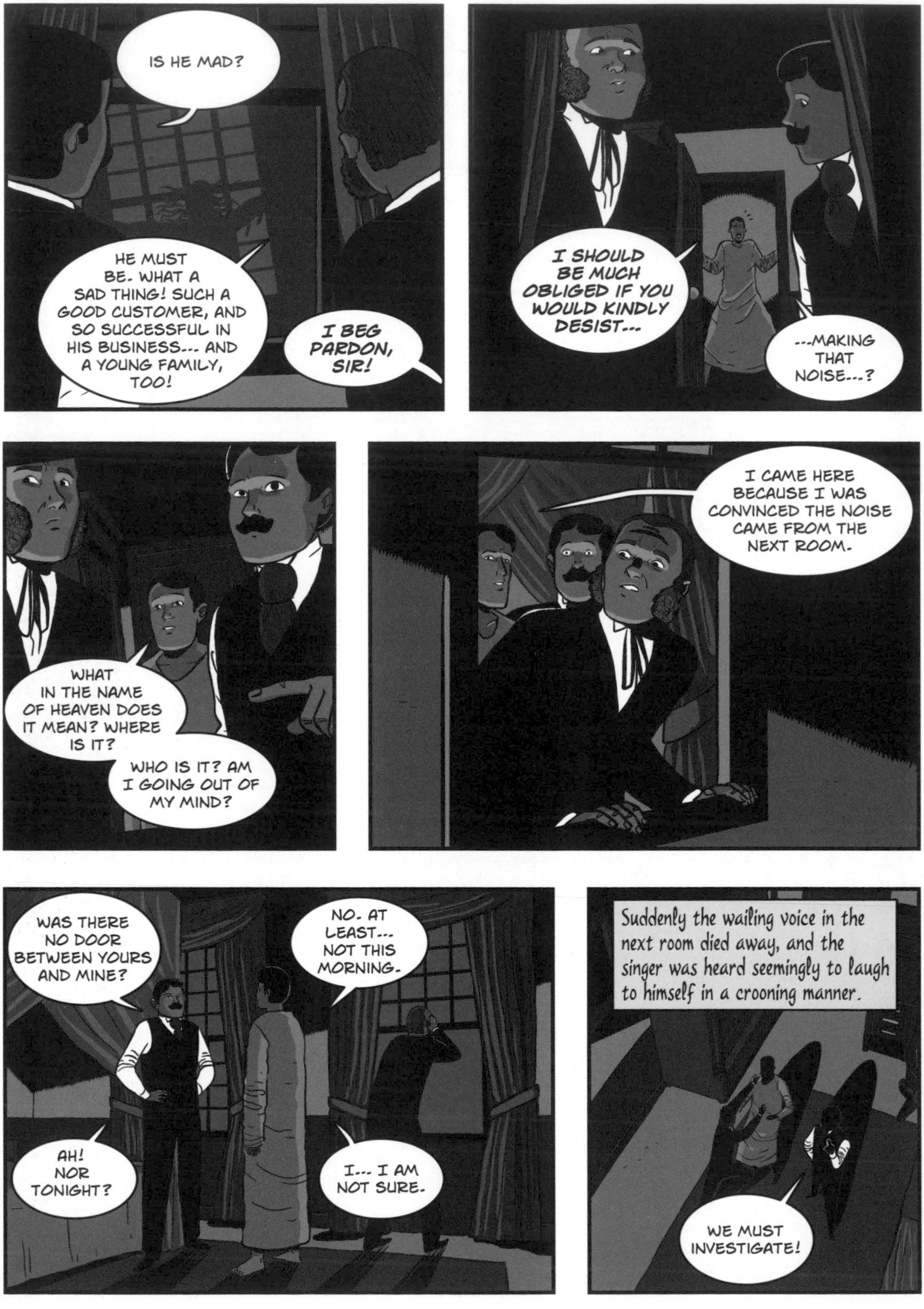
IS HE MAD?
HE MUST BE. WHAT A SAD THING! SUCH A GOOD CUSTOMER, AND SO SUCCESSFUL IN HIS BUSINESS... AND A YOUNG FAMILY, TOO!
I BEG PARDON, SIR!
I SHOULD BE MUCH OBLIGED IF YOU WOULD KINDLY DESIST...
...MAKING THAT NOISE...?
WHAT IN THE NAME OF HEAVEN DOES IT MEAN? WHERE IS IT?
WHO IS IT? AM I GOING OUT OF MY MIND?
I CAME HERE BECAUSE I WAS CONVINCED THE NOISE CAME FROM THE NEXT ROOM.
WAS THERE NO DOOR BETWEEN YOURS AND MINE?
NO. AT LEAST... NOT THIS MORNING.
AH! NOR TONIGHT?
I... I AM NOT SURE.
Suddenly the wailing voice in the next room died away, and the singer was heard seemingly to laugh to himself in a crooning manner.
WE MUST INVESTIGATE!

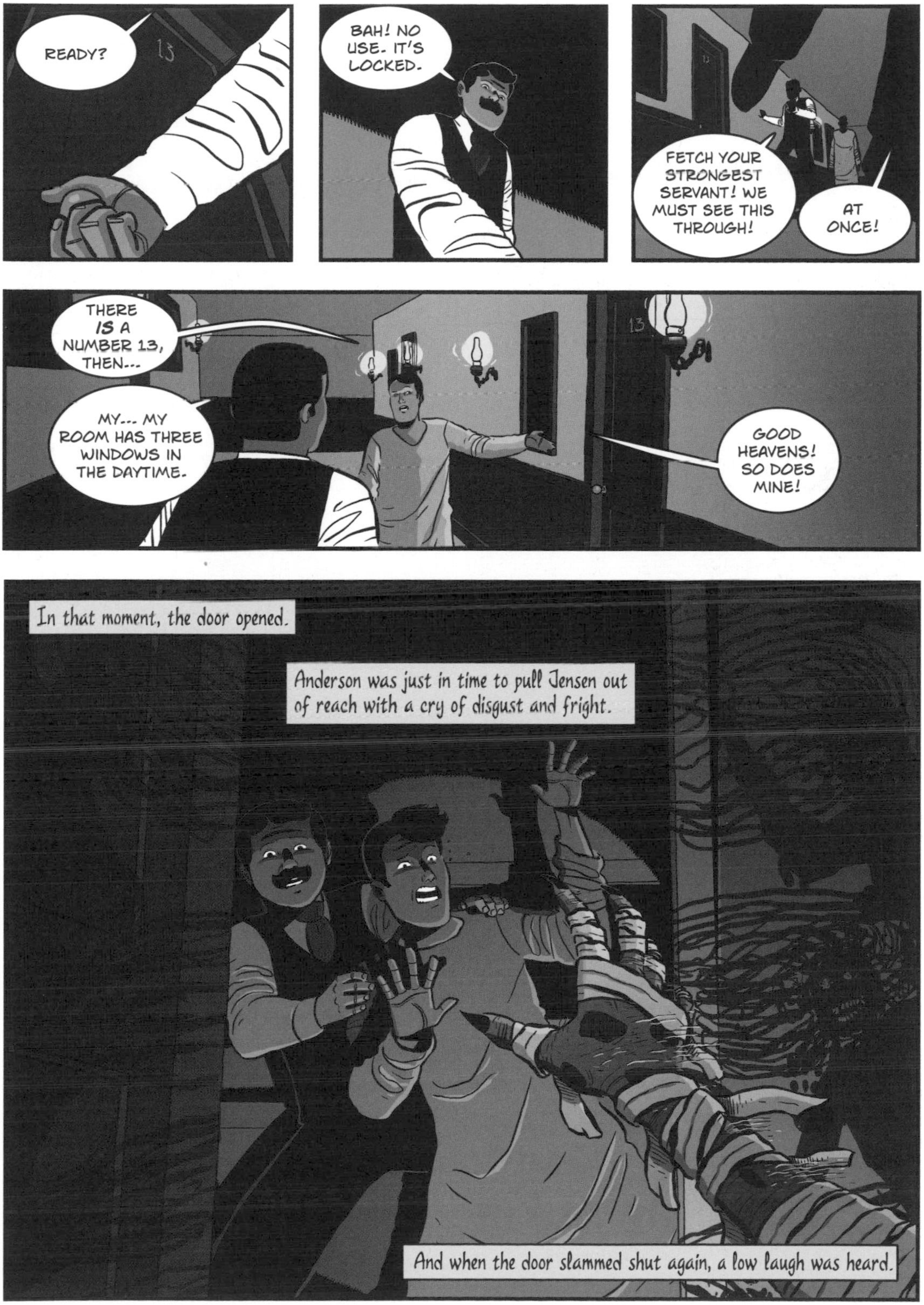
READY?
BAH! NO USE. IT'S LOCKED.
FETCH YOUR STRONGEST SERVANT! WE MUST SEE THIS THROUGH!
AT ONCE!
THERE IS A NUMBER 13, THEN...
MY... MY ROOM HAS THREE WINDOWS IN THE DAYTIME.
GOOD HEAVENS! SO DOES MINE!
In that moment, the door opened.
Anderson was just in time to pull Jensen out of reach with a cry of disgust and fright.
And when the door slammed shut again, a low laugh was heard.

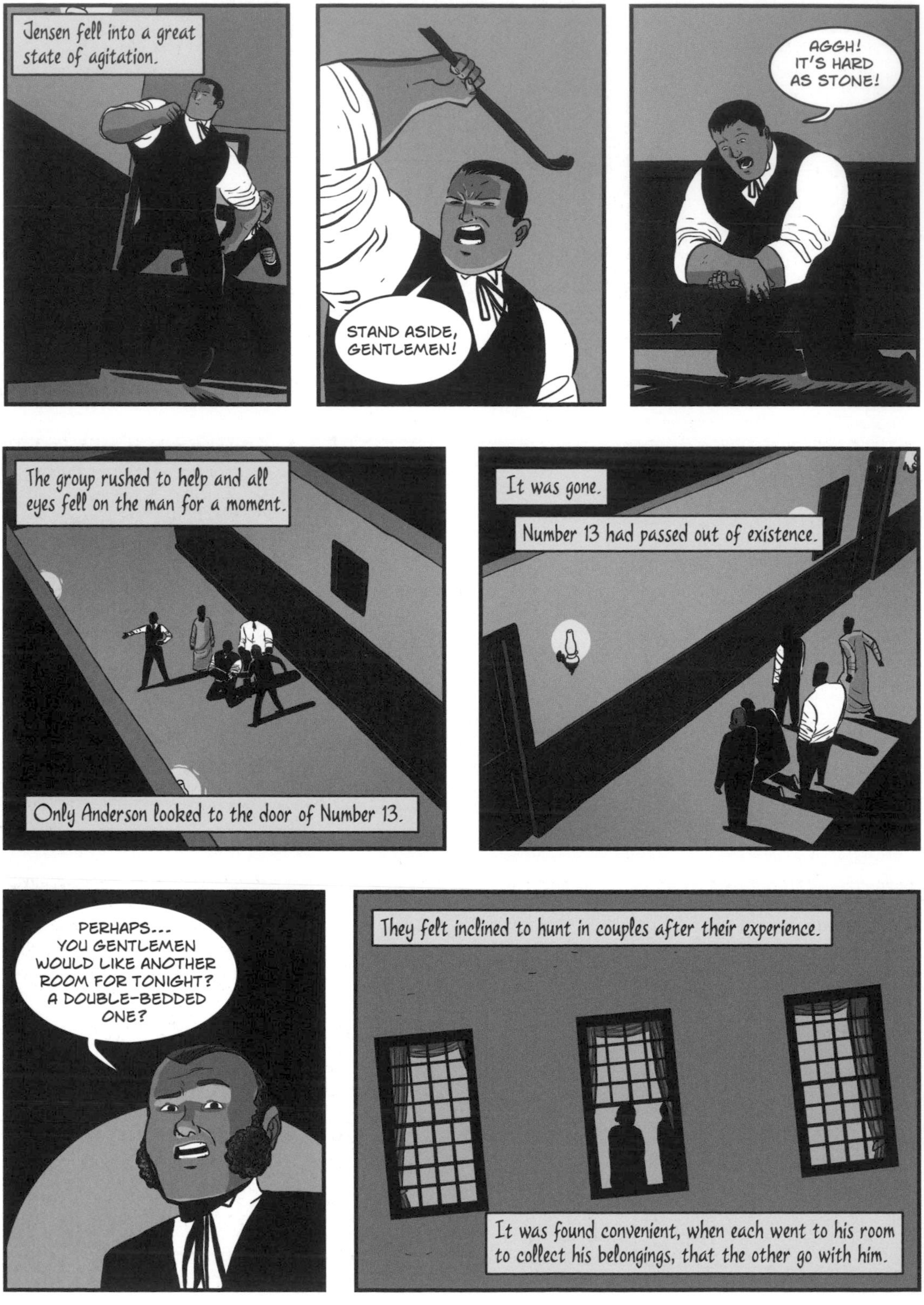
Jensen fell into a great state of agitation.
STAND ASIDE, GENTLEMEN!
AGGH! IT'S HARD AS STONE!
The group rushed to help and all eyes fell on the man for a moment.
Only Anderson looked to the door of Number 13.
It was gone.
Number 13 had passed out of existence.
PERHAPS... YOU GENTLEMEN WOULD LIKE ANOTHER ROOM FOR TONIGHT? A DOUBLE-BEDDED ONE?
They felt inclined to hunt in couples after their experience.
It was found convenient, when each went to his room to collect his belongings, that the other go with him.

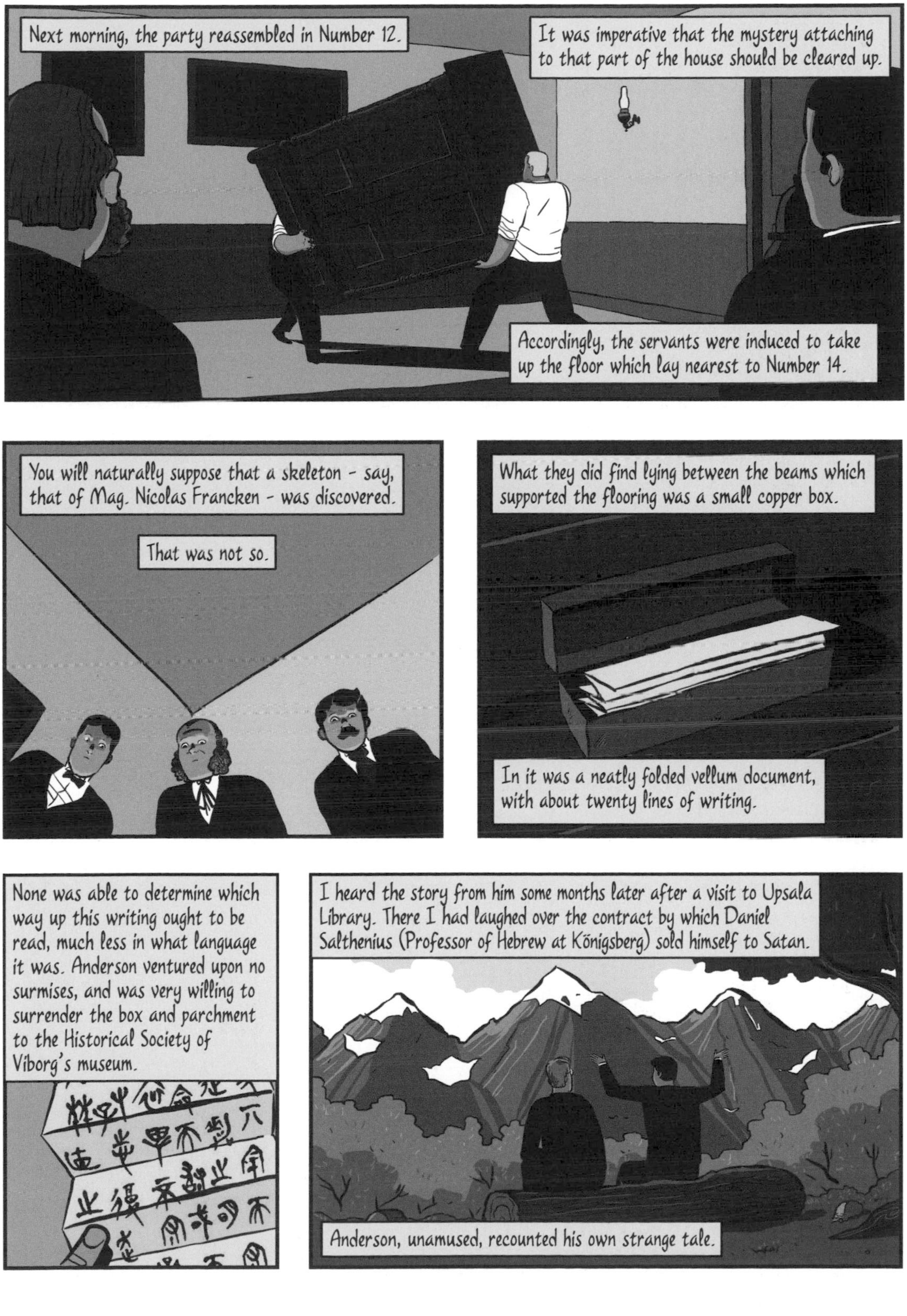
Next morning, the party reassembled in Number 12.
It was imperative that the mystery attaching to that part of the house should be cleared up.
Accordingly, the servants were induced to take up the floor which lay nearest to Number 14.
You will naturally suppose that a skeleton - say, that of Mag. Nicolas Francken - was discovered.
That was not so.
What they did find lying between the beams which supported the flooring was a small copper box.
In it was a neatly folded vellum document, with about twenty lines of writing.
None was able to determine which way up this writing ought to be read, much less in what language it was. Anderson ventured upon no surmises, and was very willing to surrender the box and parchment to the Historical Society of Viborg's museum.
I heard the story from him some months later after a visit to Upsala Library. There I had laughed over the contract by which Daniel Salthenius (Professor of Hebrew at Königsberg) sold himself to Satan.
Anderson, unamused, recounted his own strange tale.

COUNT MAGNUS

ILLUSTRATED BY ABIGAIL LARSON
COLOURS BY AL DAVISON

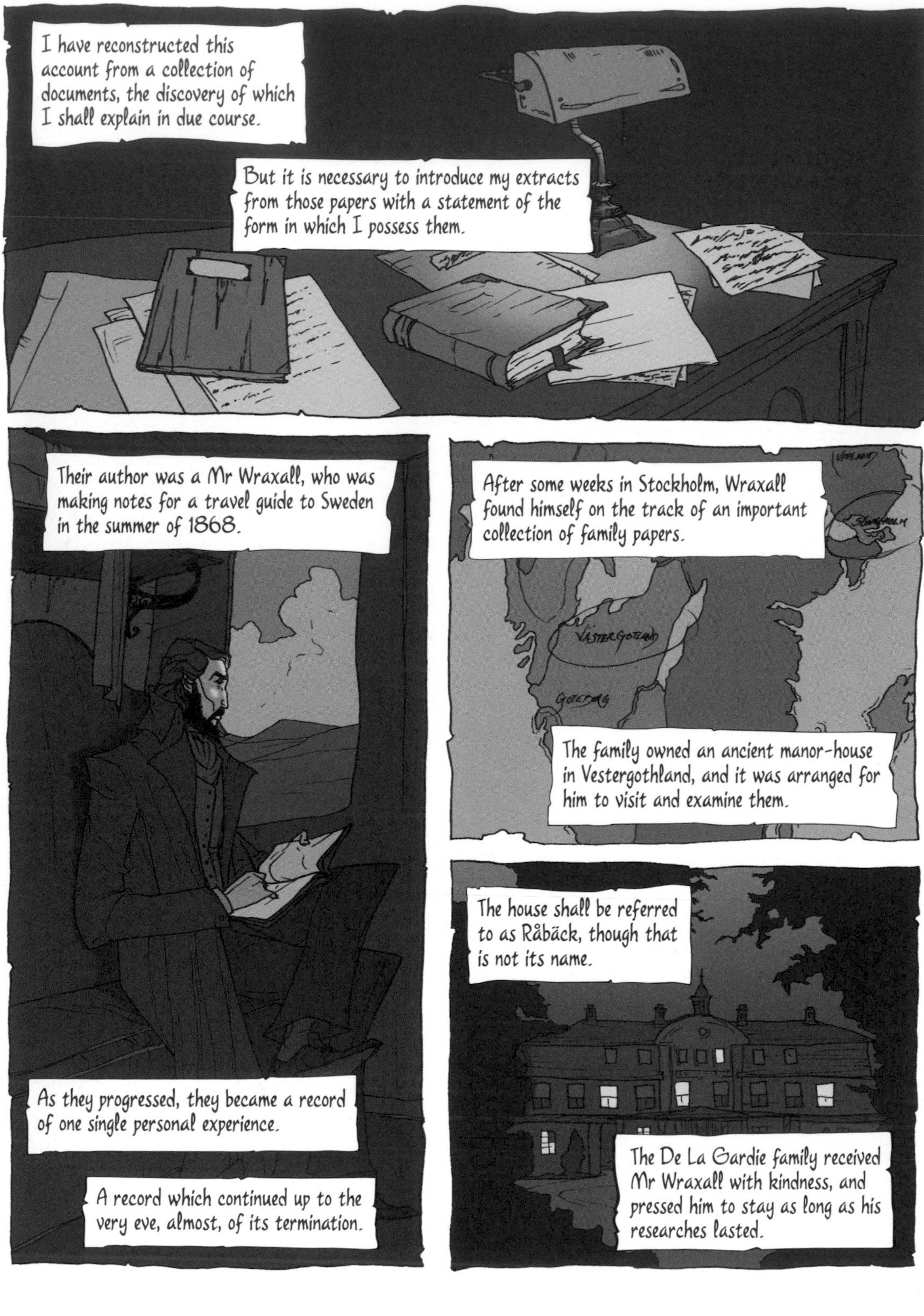
I have reconstructed this account from a collection of documents, the discovery of which I shall explain in due course.
But it is necessary to introduce my extracts from those papers with a statement of the form in which I possess them.
Their author was a Mr Wraxall, who was making notes for a travel guide to Sweden in the summer of 1868.
As they progressed, they became a record of one single personal experience.
A record which continued up to the very eve, almost, of its termination.
After some weeks in Stockholm, Wraxall found himself on the track of an important collection of family papers.
The family owned an ancient manor-house in Vestergothland, and it was arranged for him to visit and examine them.
The house shall be referred to as Råbäck, though that is not its name.
The De La Gardie family received Mr Wraxall with kindness, and pressed him to stay as long as his researches lasted.

Preferring to be independent, he settled himself at the village inn, not far from the manor-house itself.

Setting off toward Råbäck from his inn, he passed a knoll, on top of which stood a church.

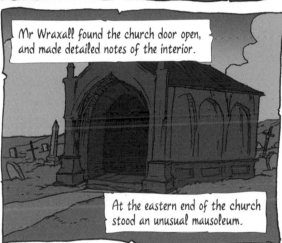

Mr Wraxall found the church door open, and made detailed notes of the interior.

At the eastern end of the church stood an unusual mausoleum.

Into this mausoleum, he could not make his way.

He could, however, see just enough to make him anxious to visit properly at a later date.

The family documents proved exceedingly interesting.

Shortly after the mansion was completed, peasants had risen and attacked several châteaux in the area, including Råbäck.

Count Magnus de la Gardie, whose portrait hung in the library, had suppressed the uprising. Documents referred to "severe punishments inflicted with no sparing hand".

INNKEEP, COULD YOU TELL ME ABOUT COUNT MAGNUS? WAS THE POPULAR ESTIMATE OF HIM *FAVOURABLE?*

It was not.

Tenants late to work were punished harshly. Houses built too close to his lands were burned. More than once Herr Nielsen mentioned that Magnus had been on the Black Pilgrimage, bringing something or someone back with him.

You will wonder what the Black Pilgrimage may have been.

But the landlord would say no more.

"If any man desires long life, a faithful messenger and the blood of his enemies..."

"...he must go into Chorazin, and there salute the prince of the air."

"(See the rest of this matter among the more private things.)"

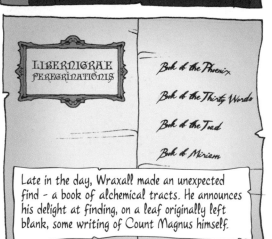

LIBERNIGRAE PEREGRINATIONIS

Book of the Phoenix

Book of the Thirty Words

Book of the Toad

Book of Miriam

Late in the day, Wraxall made an unexpected find - a book of alchemical tracts. He announces his delight at finding, on a leaf originally left blank, some writing of Count Magnus himself.

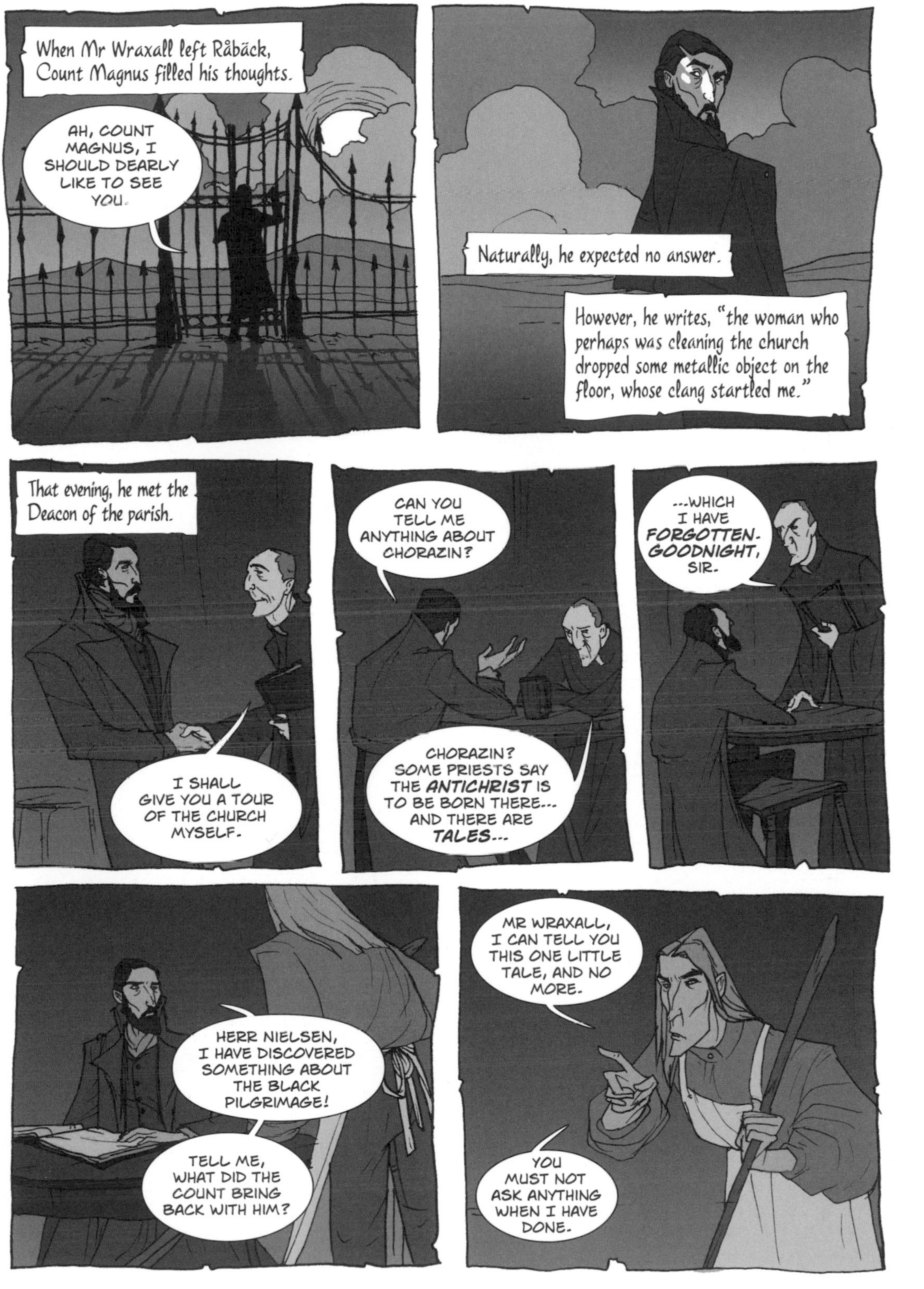
When Mr Wraxall left Råbäck, Count Magnus filled his thoughts.
AH, COUNT MAGNUS, I SHOULD DEARLY LIKE TO SEE YOU.
Naturally, he expected no answer.
However, he writes, "the woman who perhaps was cleaning the church dropped some metallic object on the floor, whose clang startled me."
That evening, he met the Deacon of the parish.
I SHALL GIVE YOU A TOUR OF THE CHURCH MYSELF.
CAN YOU TELL ME ANYTHING ABOUT CHORAZIN?
CHORAZIN? SOME PRIESTS SAY THE ANTICHRIST IS TO BE BORN THERE... AND THERE ARE TALES...
...WHICH I HAVE FORGOTTEN. GOODNIGHT, SIR.
HERR NIELSEN, I HAVE DISCOVERED SOMETHING ABOUT THE BLACK PILGRIMAGE!
TELL ME, WHAT DID THE COUNT BRING BACK WITH HIM?
MR WRAXALL, I CAN TELL YOU THIS ONE LITTLE TALE, AND NO MORE.
YOU MUST NOT ASK ANYTHING WHEN I HAVE DONE.

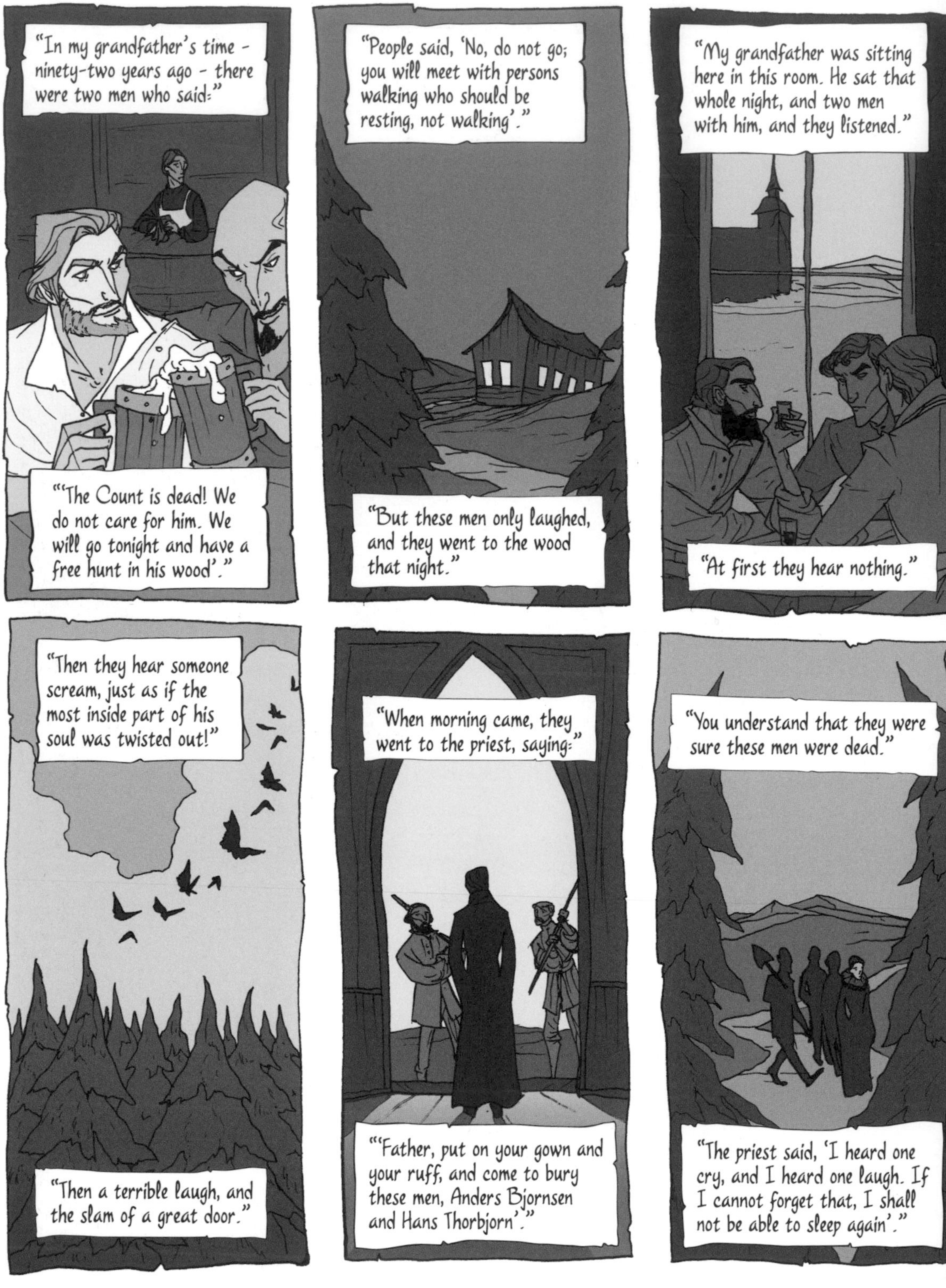
"In my grandfather's time - ninety-two years ago - there were two men who said:"
"'The Count is dead! We do not care for him. We will go tonight and have a free hunt in his wood'."
"People said, 'No, do not go; you will meet with persons walking who should be resting, not walking'."
"But these men only laughed, and they went to the wood that night."
"My grandfather was sitting here in this room. He sat that whole night, and two men with him, and they listened."
"At first they hear nothing."
"Then they hear someone scream, just as if the most inside part of his soul was twisted out!"
"Then a terrible laugh, and the slam of a great door."
"When morning came, they went to the priest, saying:"
"'Father, put on your gown and your ruff, and come to bury these men, Anders Bjornsen and Hans Thorbjorn'."
"You understand that they were sure these men were dead."
"The priest said, 'I heard one cry, and I heard one laugh. If I cannot forget that, I shall not be able to sleep again'."

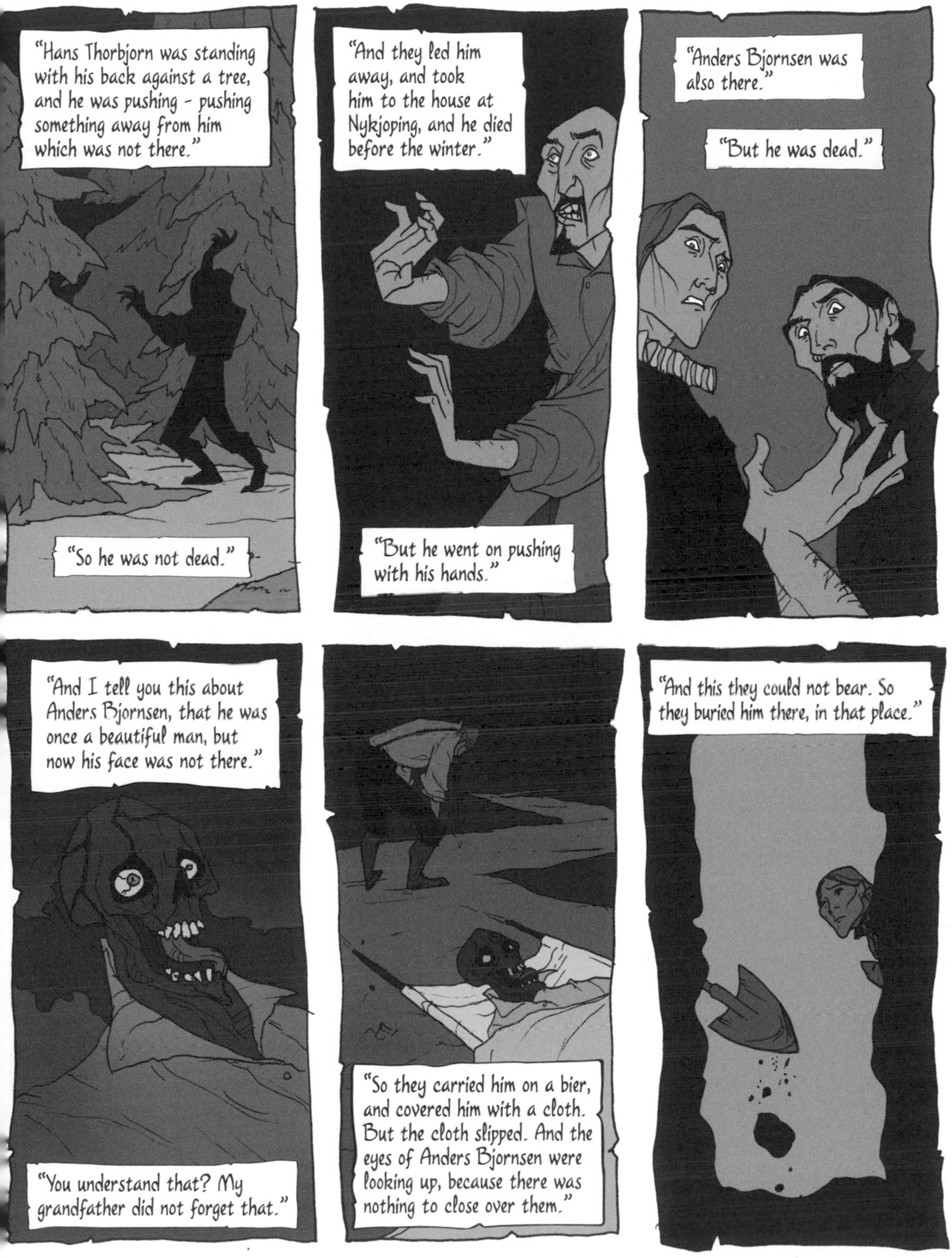
"Hans Thorbjorn was standing with his back against a tree, and he was pushing - pushing something away from him which was not there."
"So he was not dead."
"And they led him away, and took him to the house at Nykjoping, and he died before the winter."
"But he went on pushing with his hands."
"Anders Bjornsen was also there."
"But he was dead."
"And I tell you this about Anders Bjornsen, that he was once a beautiful man, but now his face was not there."
"You understand that? My grandfather did not forget that."
"So they carried him on a bier, and covered him with a cloth. But the cloth slipped. And the eyes of Anders Bjornsen were looking up, because there was nothing to close over them."
"And this they could not bear. So they buried him there, in that place."

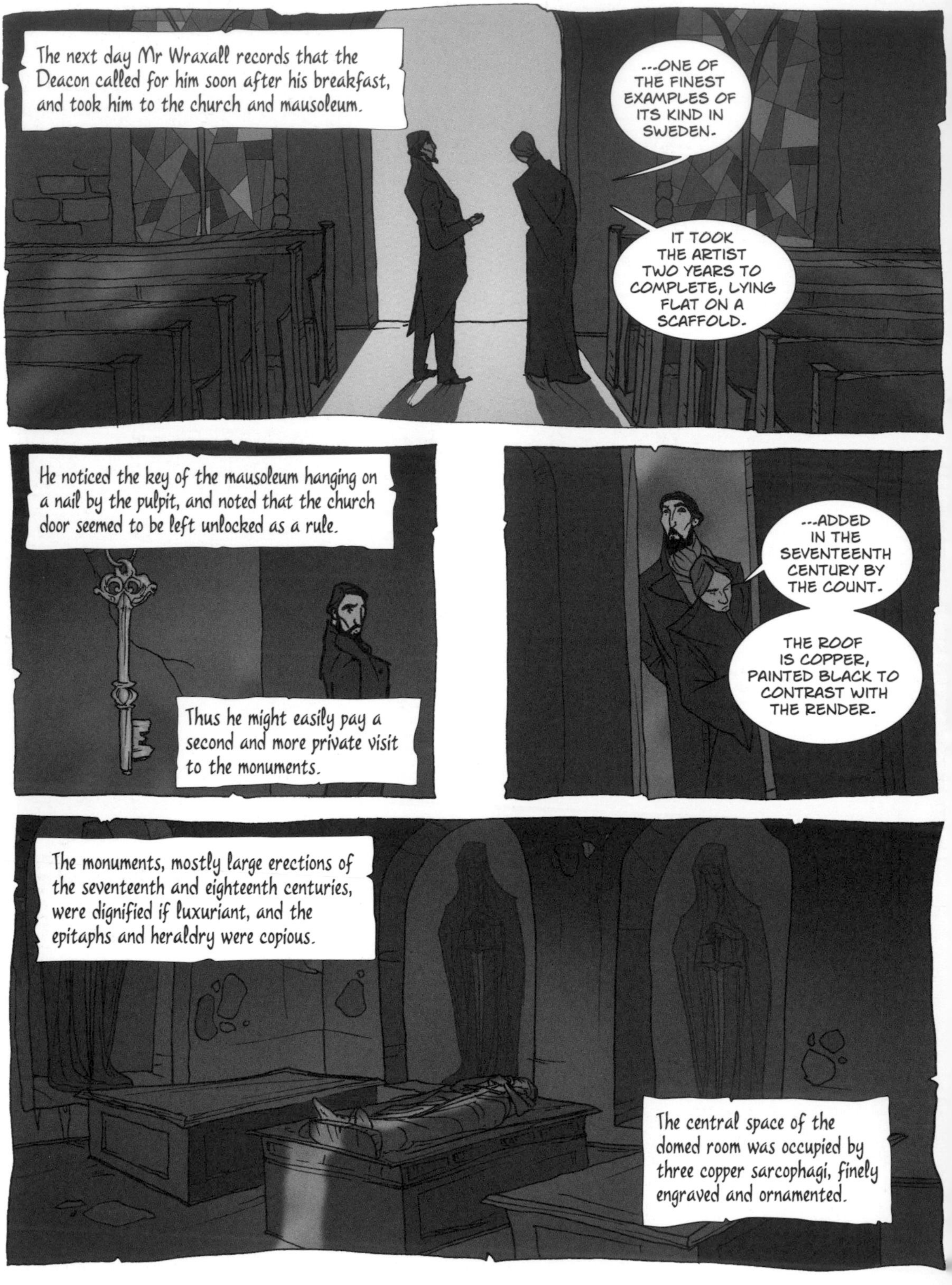

The next day Mr Wraxall records that the Deacon called for him soon after his breakfast, and took him to the church and mausoleum.
---ONE OF THE FINEST EXAMPLES OF ITS KIND IN SWEDEN.
IT TOOK THE ARTIST TWO YEARS TO COMPLETE, LYING FLAT ON A SCAFFOLD.
He noticed the key of the mausoleum hanging on a nail by the pulpit, and noted that the church door seemed to be left unlocked as a rule.
Thus he might easily pay a second and more private visit to the monuments.
---ADDED IN THE SEVENTEENTH CENTURY BY THE COUNT.
THE ROOF IS COPPER, PAINTED BLACK TO CONTRAST WITH THE RENDER.
The monuments, mostly large erections of the seventeenth and eighteenth centuries, were dignified if luxuriant, and the epitaphs and heraldry were copious.
The central space of the domed room was occupied by three copper sarcophagi, finely engraved and ornamented.

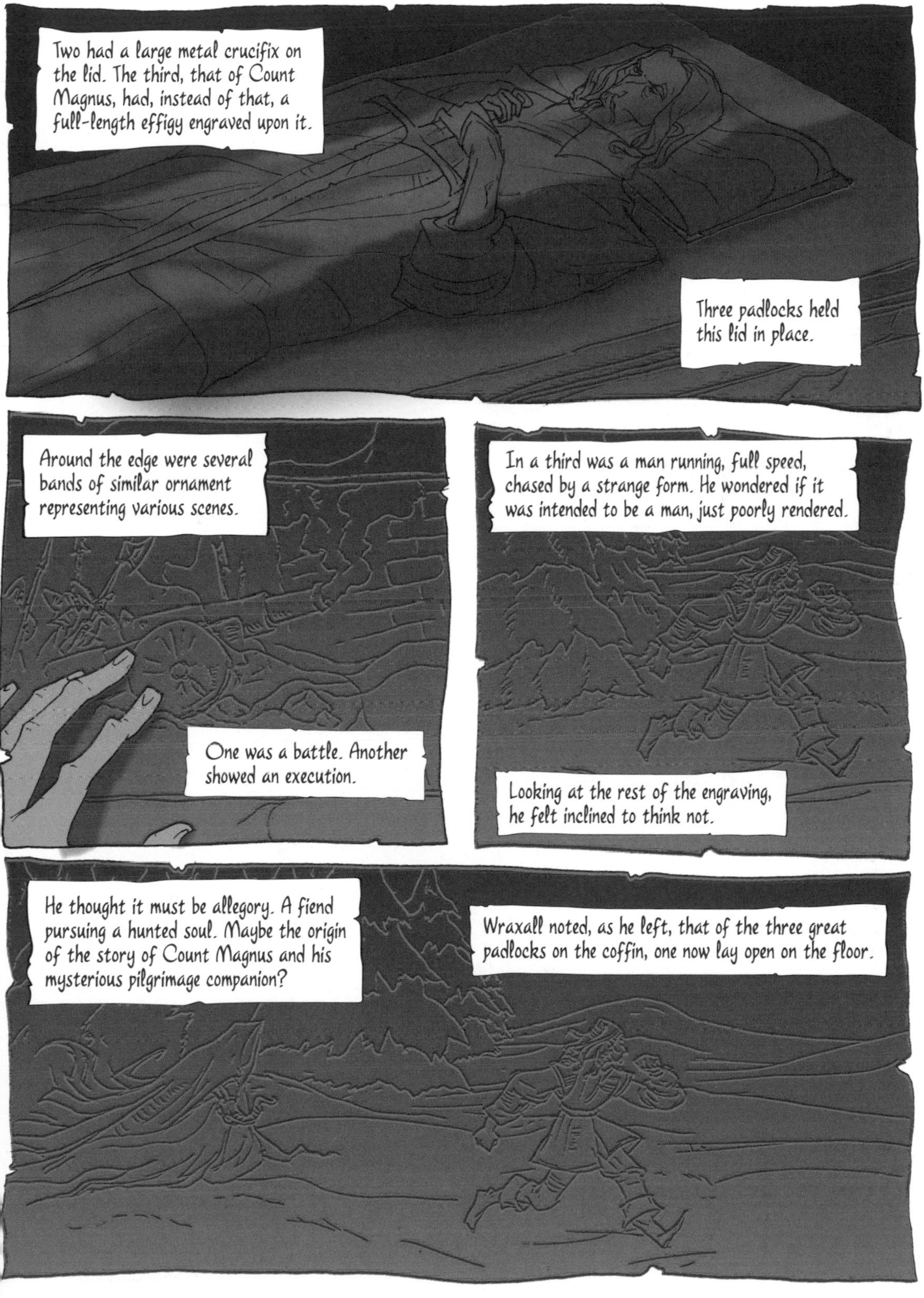
Two had a large metal crucifix on the lid. The third, that of Count Magnus, had, instead of that, a full-length effigy engraved upon it.
Three padlocks held this lid in place.
Around the edge were several bands of similar ornament representing various scenes.
One was a battle. Another showed an execution.
In a third was a man running, full speed, chased by a strange form. He wondered if it was intended to be a man, just poorly rendered.
Looking at the rest of the engraving, he felt inclined to think not.
He thought it must be allegory. A fiend pursuing a hunted soul. Maybe the origin of the story of Count Magnus and his mysterious pilgrimage companion?
Wraxall noted, as he left, that of the three great padlocks on the coffin, one now lay open on the floor.

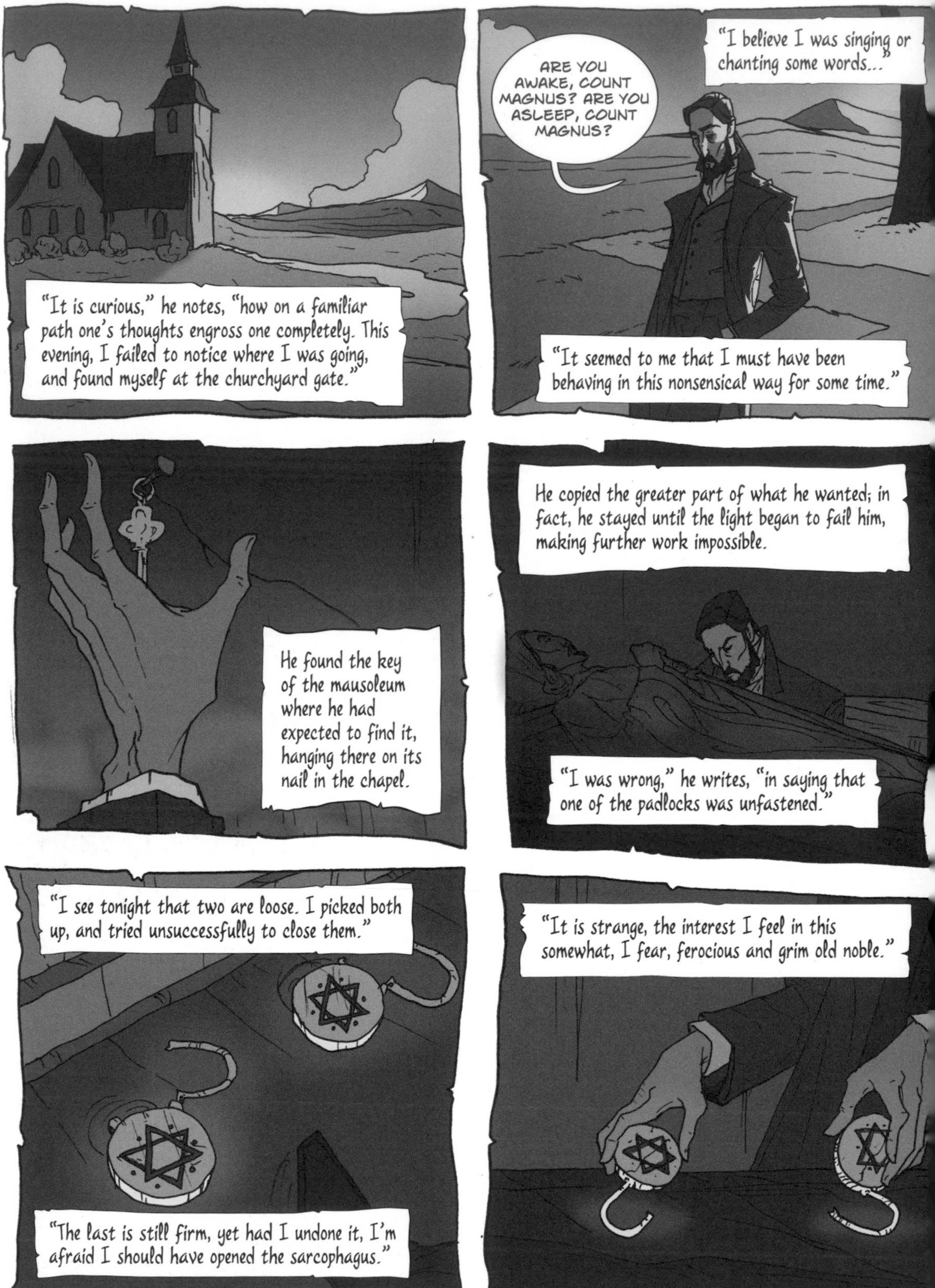
"It is curious," he notes, "how on a familiar path one's thoughts engross one completely. This evening, I failed to notice where I was going, and found myself at the churchyard gate."
"I believe I was singing or chanting some words..."
ARE YOU AWAKE, COUNT MAGNUS? ARE YOU ASLEEP, COUNT MAGNUS?
"It seemed to me that I must have been behaving in this nonsensical way for some time."
He found the key of the mausoleum where he had expected to find it, hanging there on its nail in the chapel.
He copied the greater part of what he wanted; in fact, he stayed until the light began to fail him, making further work impossible.
"I was wrong," he writes, "in saying that one of the padlocks was unfastened."
"I see tonight that two are loose. I picked both up, and tried unsuccessfully to close them."
"The last is still firm, yet had I undone it, I'm afraid I should have opened the sarcophagus."
"It is strange, the interest I feel in this somewhat, I fear, ferocious and grim old noble."

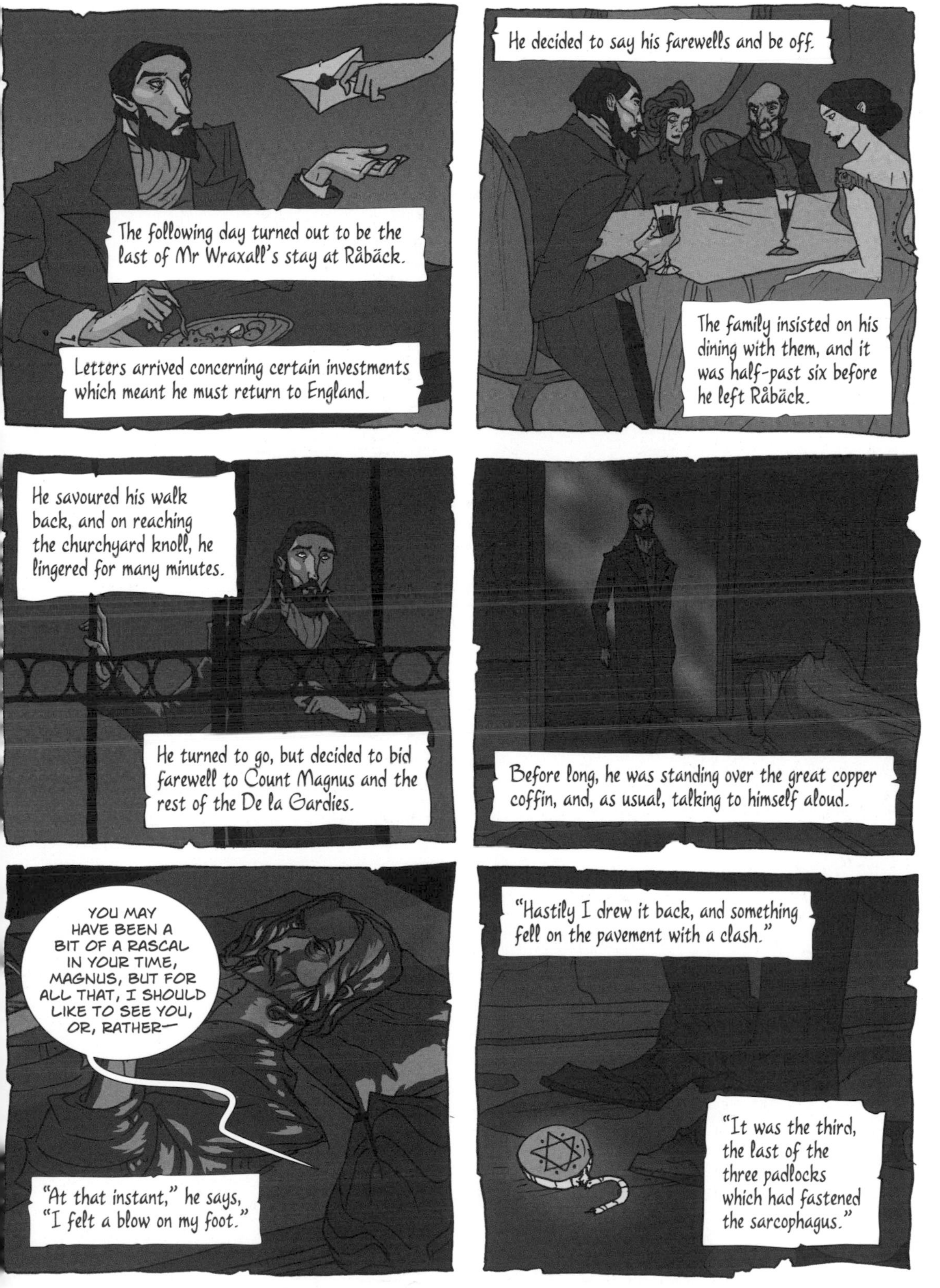
The following day turned out to be the last of Mr Wraxall's stay at Råbäck.
Letters arrived concerning certain investments which meant he must return to England.
He decided to say his farewells and be off.
The family insisted on his dining with them, and it was half-past six before he left Råbäck.
He savoured his walk back, and on reaching the churchyard knoll, he lingered for many minutes.
He turned to go, but decided to bid farewell to Count Magnus and the rest of the De la Gardies.
Before long, he was standing over the great copper coffin, and, as usual, talking to himself aloud.
YOU MAY HAVE BEEN A BIT OF A RASCAL IN YOUR TIME, MAGNUS, BUT FOR ALL THAT, I SHOULD LIKE TO SEE YOU, OR, RATHER—
"At that instant," he says, "I felt a blow on my foot."
"Hastily I drew it back, and something fell on the pavement with a clash."
"It was the third, the last of the three padlocks which had fastened the sarcophagus."

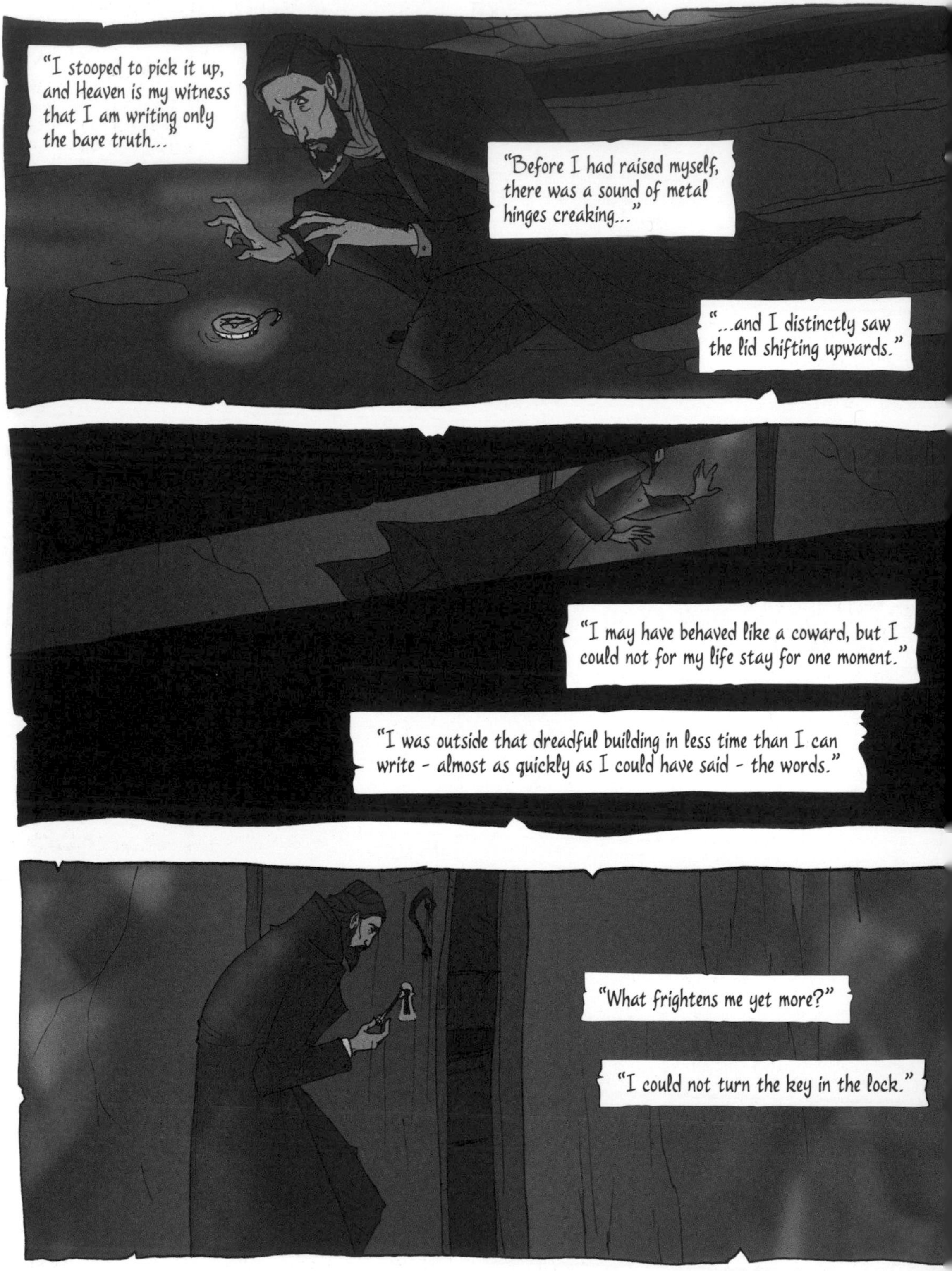
"I stooped to pick it up, and Heaven is my witness that I am writing only the bare truth..."
"Before I had raised myself, there was a sound of metal hinges creaking..."
"...and I distinctly saw the lid shifting upwards."
"I may have behaved like a coward, but I could not for my life stay for one moment."
"I was outside that dreadful building in less time than I can write - almost as quickly as I could have said - the words."
"What frightens me yet more?"
"I could not turn the key in the lock."

"As I sit here in my room noting these facts, I ask myself (it was not twenty minutes ago) whether that noise of creaking metal continued."

"I cannot tell whether it did or not."

"I only know that there was something more than I have written that alarmed me..."

"...but whether it was sound or sight I am not able to remember."

"If only I could remember..."

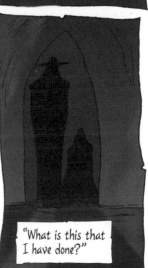

"What is this that I have done?"

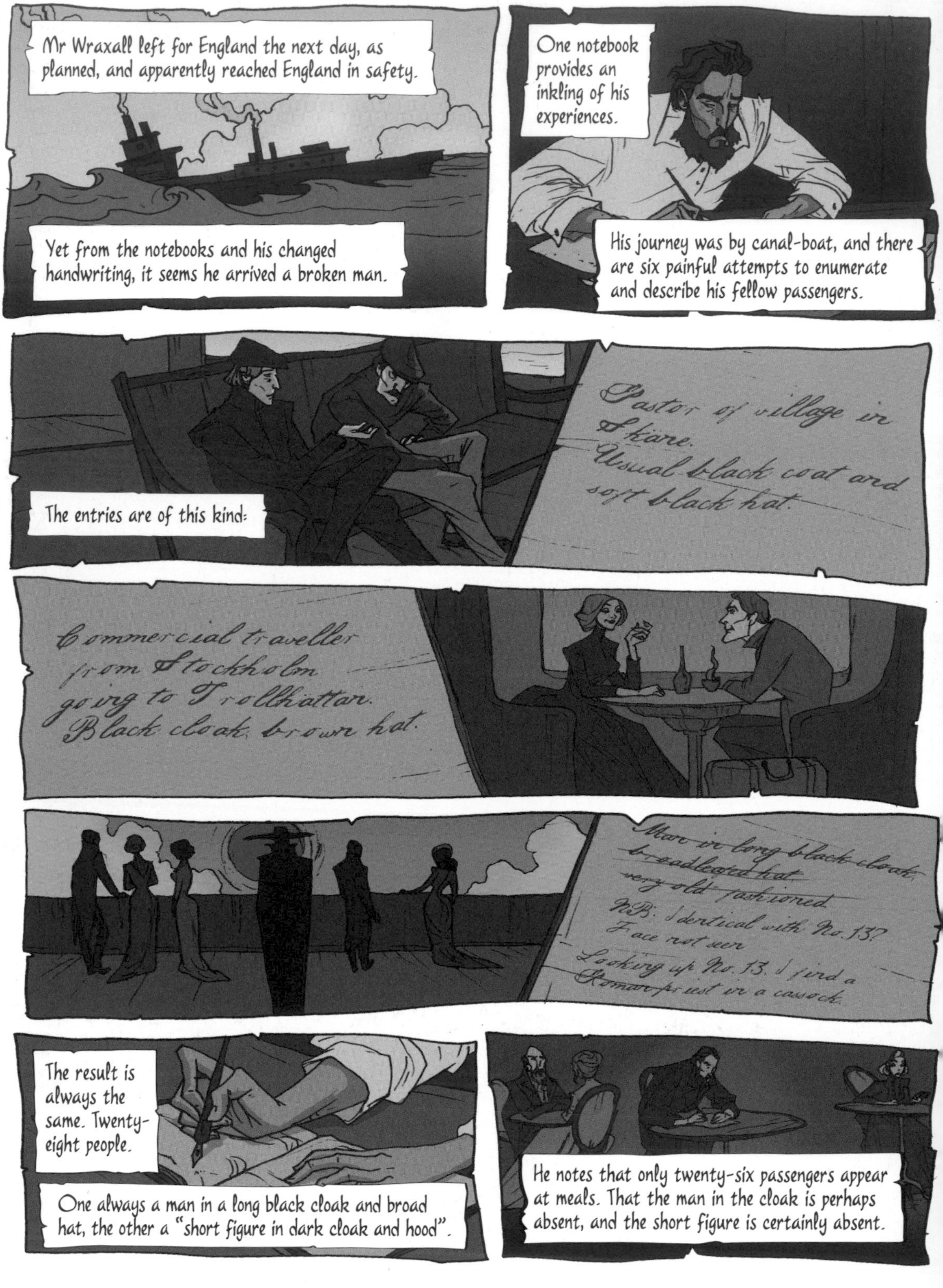
Mr Wraxall left for England the next day, as planned, and apparently reached England in safety.
Yet from the notebooks and his changed handwriting, it seems he arrived a broken man.
One notebook provides an inkling of his experiences.
His journey was by canal-boat, and there are six painful attempts to enumerate and describe his fellow passengers.
The entries are of this kind:
Pastor of village in Skäne. Usual black coat and soft black hat.
Commercial traveller from Stockholm going to Trollhättan. Black cloak, brown hat.
Man in long black cloak, broadleafed hat, very old-fashioned.
NB: Identical with No. 13? Face not seen
Looking up No. 13, I find a Roman priest in a cassock.
The result is always the same. Twenty-eight people.
One always a man in a long black cloak and broad hat, the other a "short figure in dark cloak and hood".
He notes that only twenty-six passengers appear at meals. That the man in the cloak is perhaps absent, and the short figure is certainly absent.

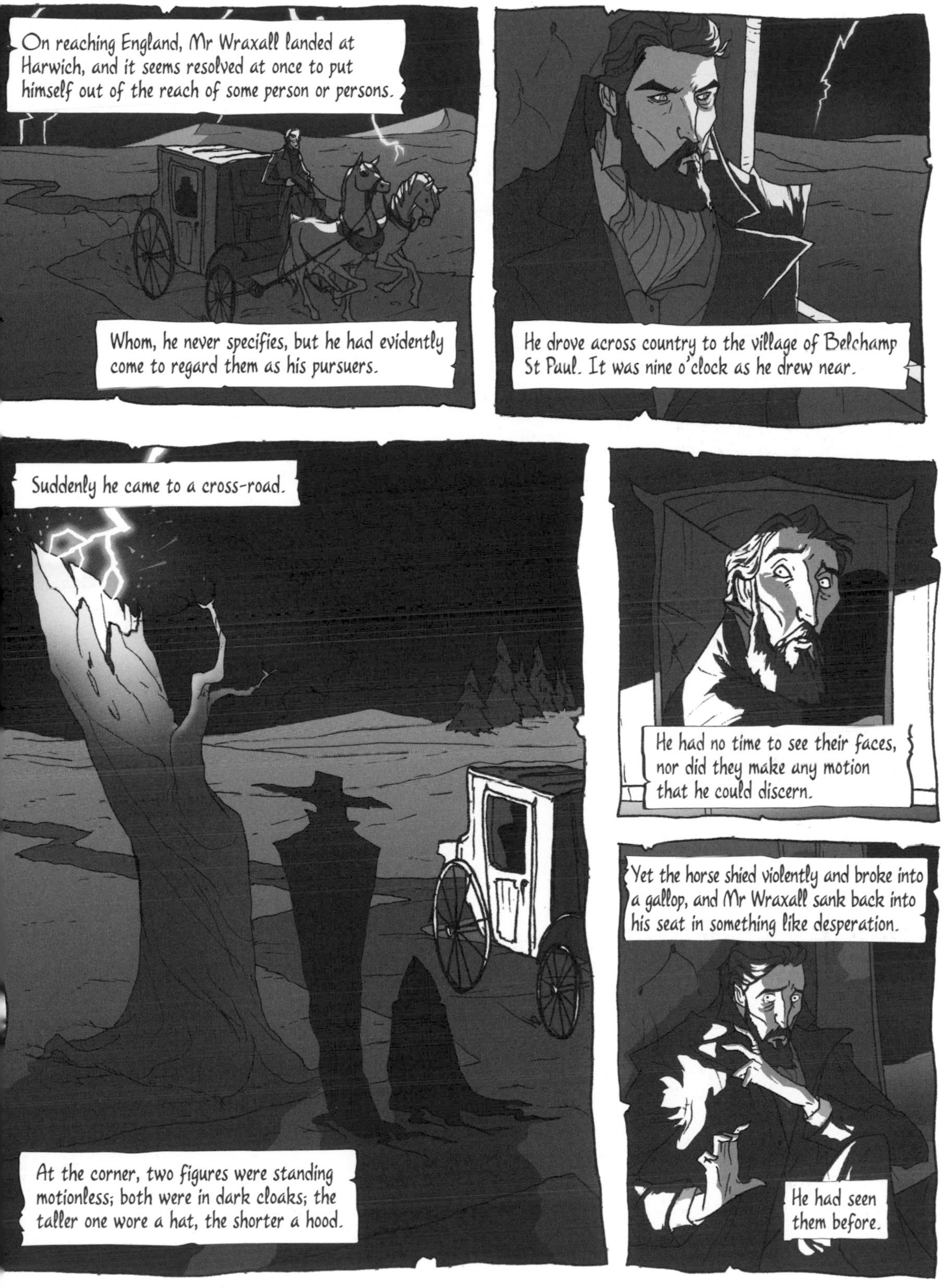
On reaching England, Mr Wraxall landed at Harwich, and it seems resolved at once to put himself out of the reach of some person or persons.
Whom, he never specifies, but he had evidently come to regard them as his pursuers.
He drove across country to the village of Belchamp St Paul. It was nine o'clock as he drew near.
Suddenly he came to a cross-road.
At the corner, two figures were standing motionless; both were in dark cloaks; the taller one wore a hat, the shorter a hood.
He had no time to see their faces, nor did they make any motion that he could discern.
Yet the horse shied violently and broke into a gallop, and Mr Wraxall sank back into his seat in something like desperation.
He had seen them before.

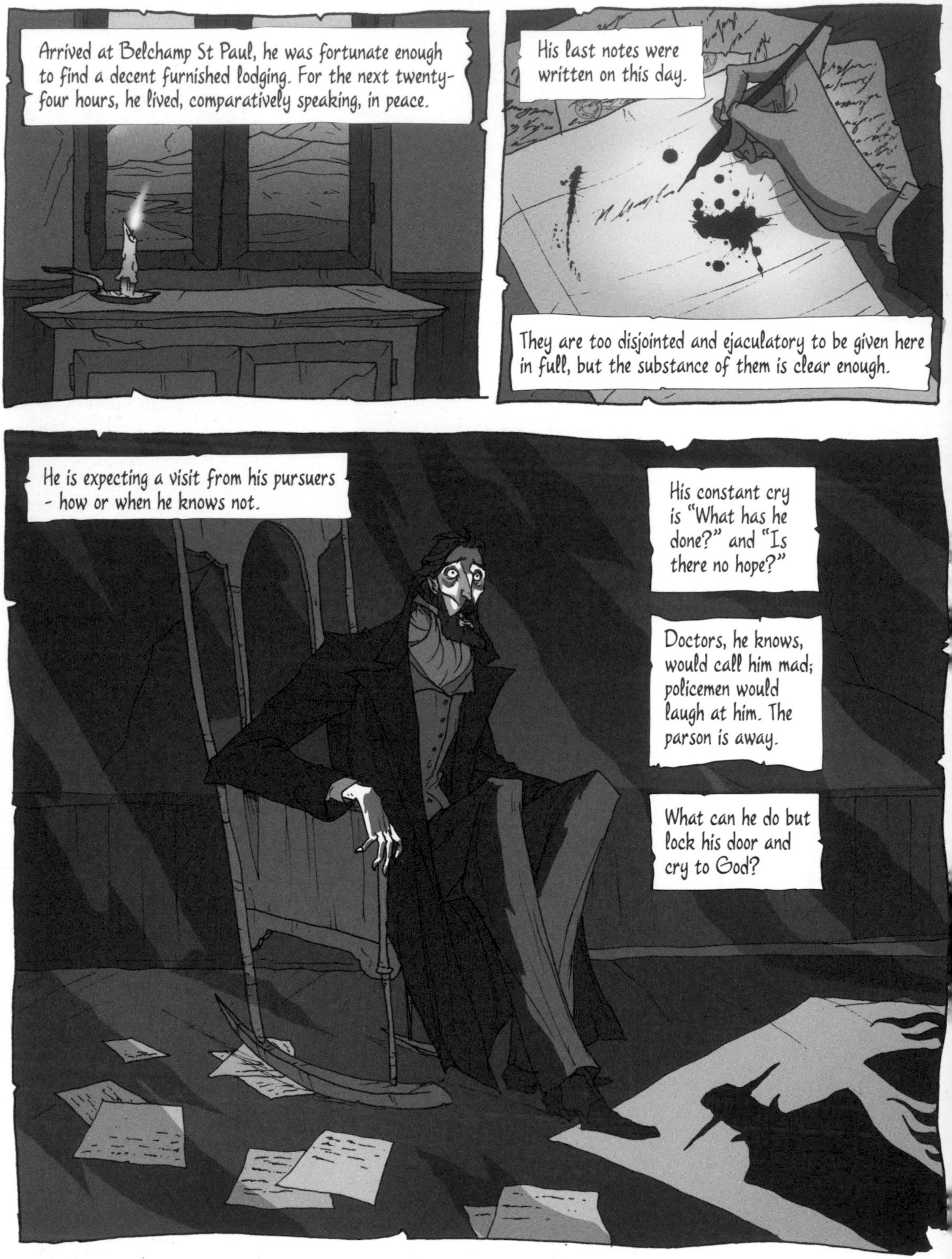
Arrived at Belchamp St Paul, he was fortunate enough to find a decent furnished lodging. For the next twenty-four hours, he lived, comparatively speaking, in peace.
His last notes were written on this day.
They are too disjointed and ejaculatory to be given here in full, but the substance of them is clear enough.
He is expecting a visit from his pursuers - how or when he knows not.
His constant cry is "What has he done?" and "Is there no hope?"
Doctors, he knows, would call him mad; policemen would laugh at him. The parson is away.
What can he do but lock his door and cry to God?

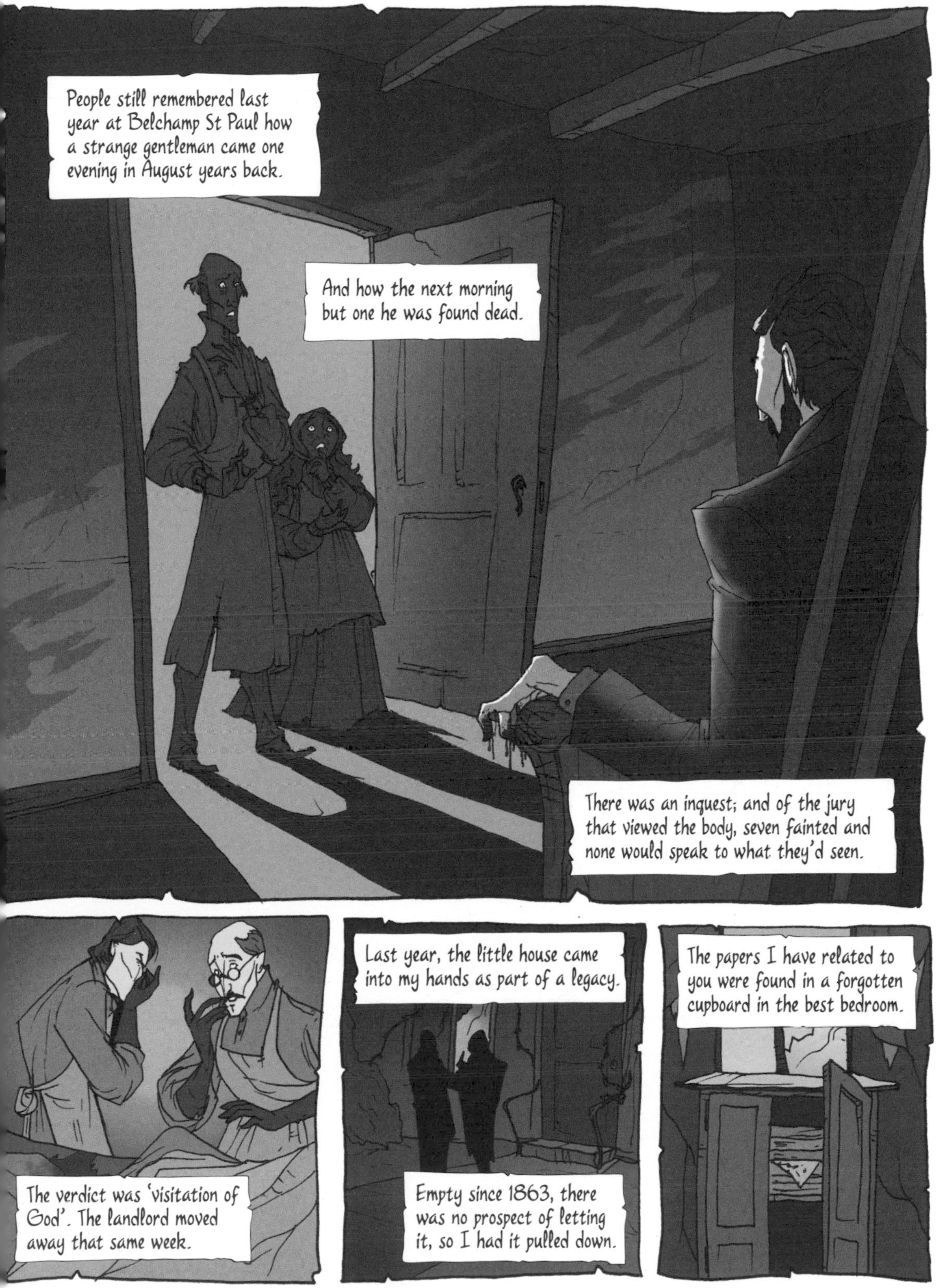
People still remembered last year at Belchamp St Paul how a strange gentleman came one evening in August years back.
And how the next morning but one he was found dead.
There was an inquest; and of the jury that viewed the body, seven fainted and none would speak to what they'd seen.
The verdict was 'visitation of God'. The landlord moved away that same week.
Last year, the little house came into my hands as part of a legacy.
Empty since 1863, there was no prospect of letting it, so I had it pulled down.
The papers I have related to you were found in a forgotten cupboard in the best bedroom.

'OH, WHISTLE, AND I'LL COME TO YOU, MY LAD'

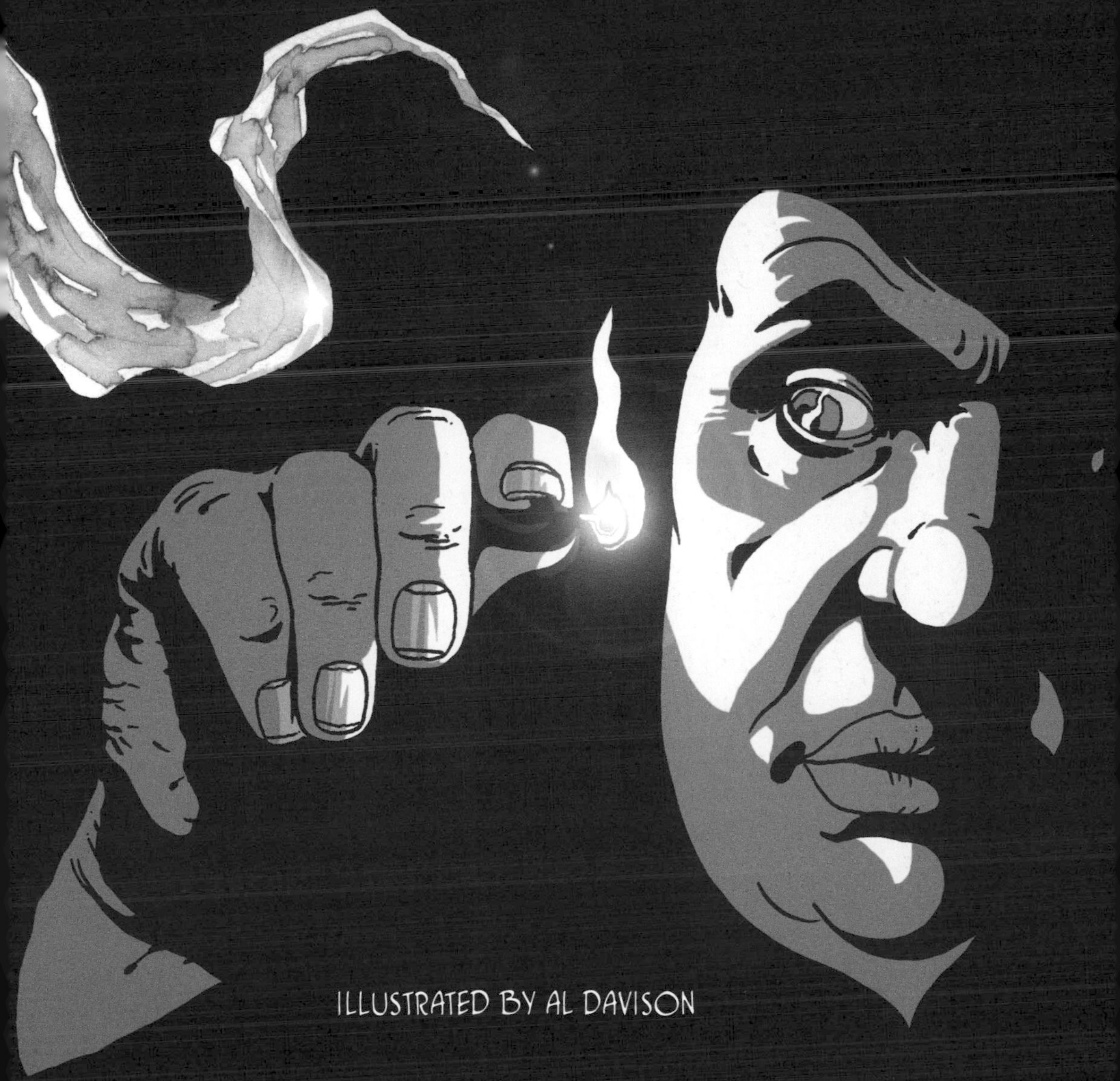

ILLUSTRATED BY AL DAVISON

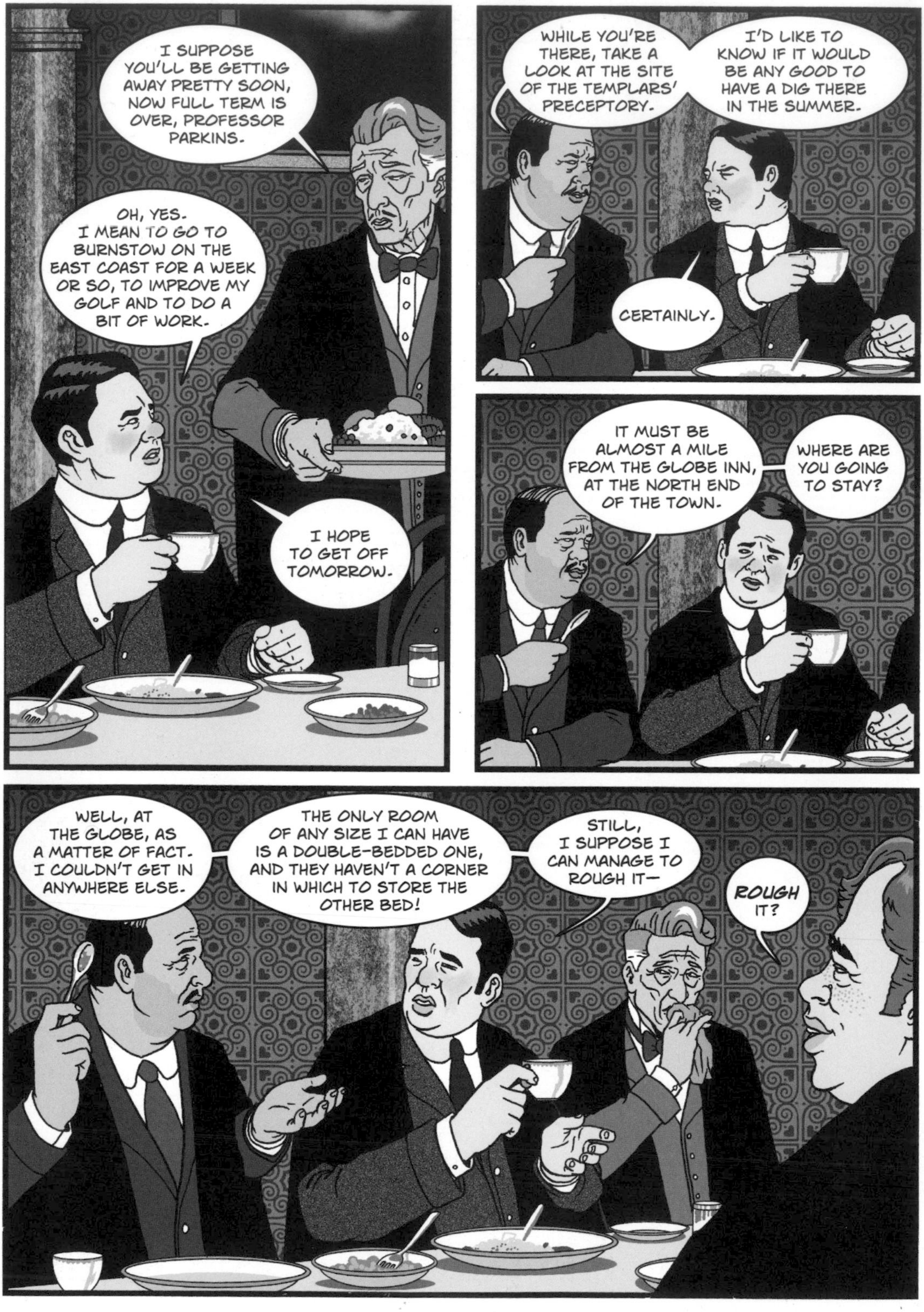
I SUPPOSE YOU'LL BE GETTING AWAY PRETTY SOON, NOW FULL TERM IS OVER, PROFESSOR PARKINS.
OH, YES. I MEAN TO GO TO BURNSTOW ON THE EAST COAST FOR A WEEK OR SO, TO IMPROVE MY GOLF AND TO DO A BIT OF WORK.
I HOPE TO GET OFF TOMORROW.
WHILE YOU'RE THERE, TAKE A LOOK AT THE SITE OF THE TEMPLARS' PRECEPTORY.
I'D LIKE TO KNOW IF IT WOULD BE ANY GOOD TO HAVE A DIG THERE IN THE SUMMER.
CERTAINLY.
WHERE ARE YOU GOING TO STAY?
IT MUST BE ALMOST A MILE FROM THE GLOBE INN, AT THE NORTH END OF THE TOWN.
WELL, AT THE GLOBE, AS A MATTER OF FACT. I COULDN'T GET IN ANYWHERE ELSE.
THE ONLY ROOM OF ANY SIZE I CAN HAVE IS A DOUBLE-BEDDED ONE, AND THEY HAVEN'T A CORNER IN WHICH TO STORE THE OTHER BED!
STILL, I SUPPOSE I CAN MANAGE TO ROUGH IT—
ROUGH IT?

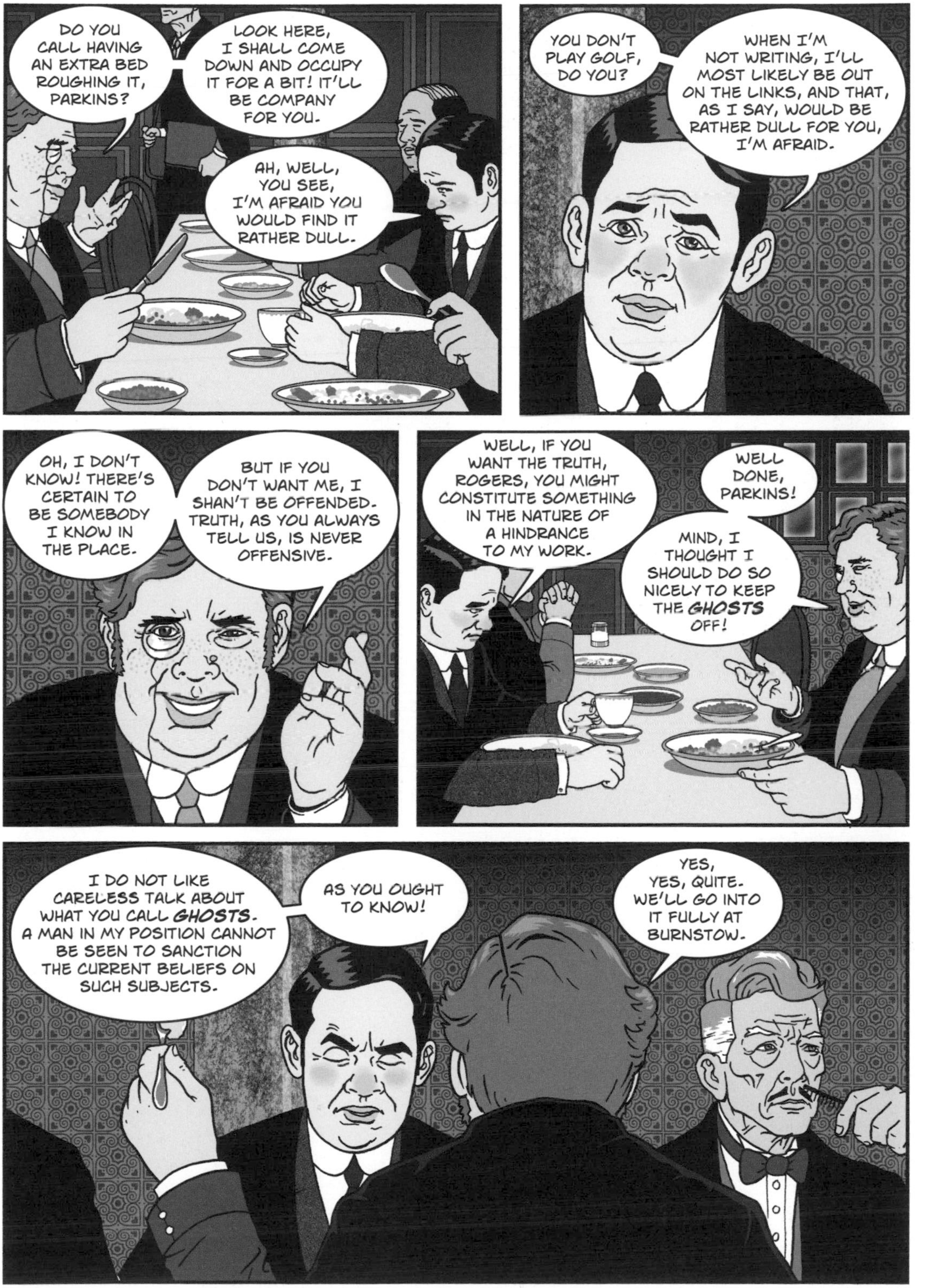
DO YOU CALL HAVING AN EXTRA BED ROUGHING IT, PARKINS?
LOOK HERE, I SHALL COME DOWN AND OCCUPY IT FOR A BIT! IT'LL BE COMPANY FOR YOU.
AH, WELL, YOU SEE, I'M AFRAID YOU WOULD FIND IT RATHER DULL.
YOU DON'T PLAY GOLF, DO YOU?
WHEN I'M NOT WRITING, I'LL MOST LIKELY BE OUT ON THE LINKS, AND THAT, AS I SAY, WOULD BE RATHER DULL FOR YOU, I'M AFRAID.
OH, I DON'T KNOW! THERE'S CERTAIN TO BE SOMEBODY I KNOW IN THE PLACE.
BUT IF YOU DON'T WANT ME, I SHAN'T BE OFFENDED. TRUTH, AS YOU ALWAYS TELL US, IS NEVER OFFENSIVE.
WELL, IF YOU WANT THE TRUTH, ROGERS, YOU MIGHT CONSTITUTE SOMETHING IN THE NATURE OF A HINDRANCE TO MY WORK.
WELL DONE, PARKINS!
MIND, I THOUGHT I SHOULD DO SO NICELY TO KEEP THE **GHOSTS** OFF!
I DO NOT LIKE CARELESS TALK ABOUT WHAT YOU CALL **GHOSTS**. A MAN IN MY POSITION CANNOT BE SEEN TO SANCTION THE CURRENT BELIEFS ON SUCH SUBJECTS.
AS YOU OUGHT TO KNOW!
YES, YES, QUITE. WE'LL GO INTO IT FULLY AT BURNSTOW.

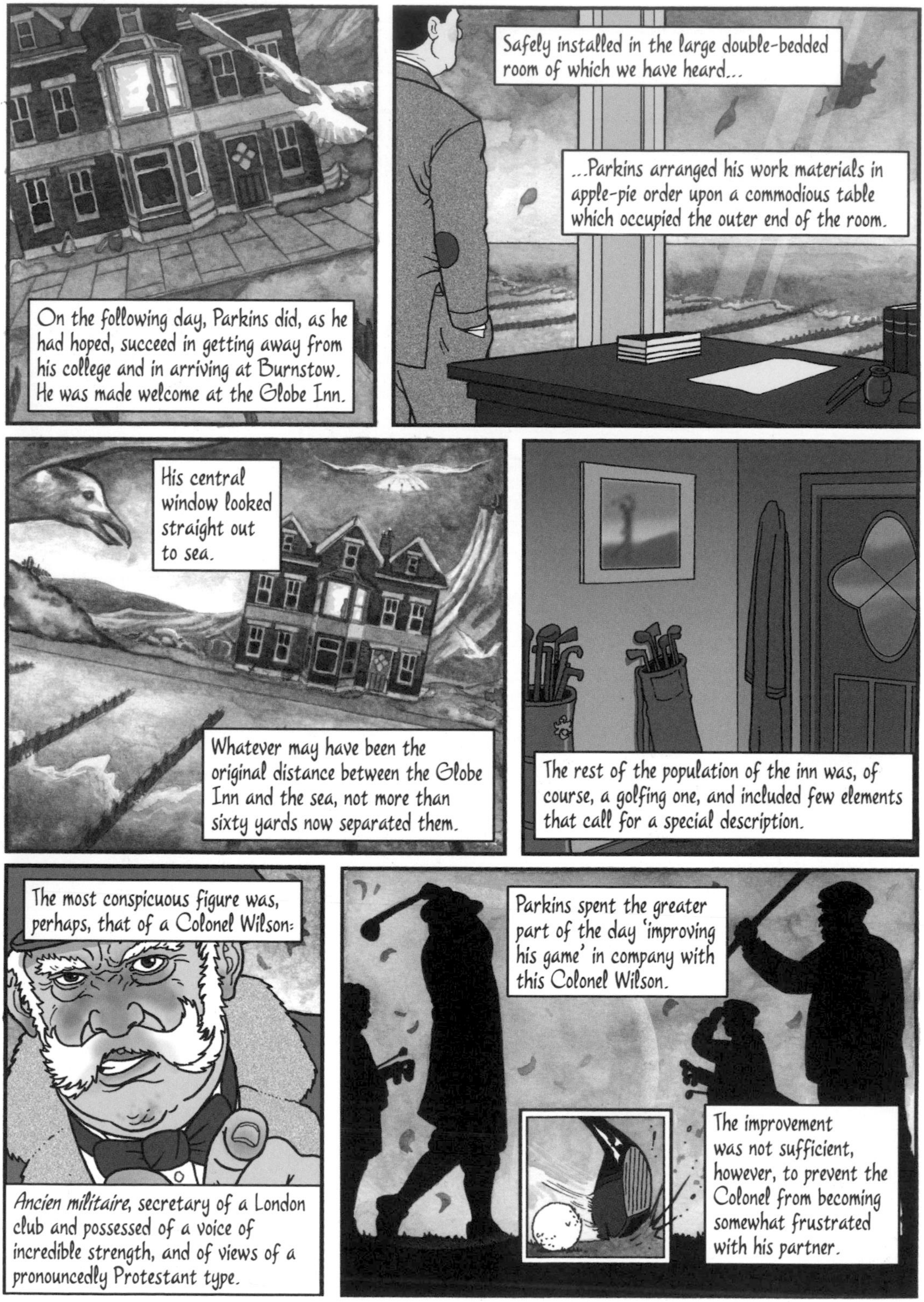
On the following day, Parkins did, as he had hoped, succeed in getting away from his college and in arriving at Burnstow. He was made welcome at the Globe Inn.
Safely installed in the large double-bedded room of which we have heard...
...Parkins arranged his work materials in apple-pie order upon a commodious table which occupied the outer end of the room.
His central window looked straight out to sea.
Whatever may have been the original distance between the Globe Inn and the sea, not more than sixty yards now separated them.
The rest of the population of the inn was, of course, a golfing one, and included few elements that call for a special description.
The most conspicuous figure was, perhaps, that of a Colonel Wilson:
Ancien militaire, secretary of a London club and possessed of a voice of incredible strength, and of views of a pronouncedly Protestant type.
Parkins spent the greater part of the day 'improving his game' in company with this Colonel Wilson.
The improvement was not sufficient, however, to prevent the Colonel from becoming somewhat frustrated with his partner.

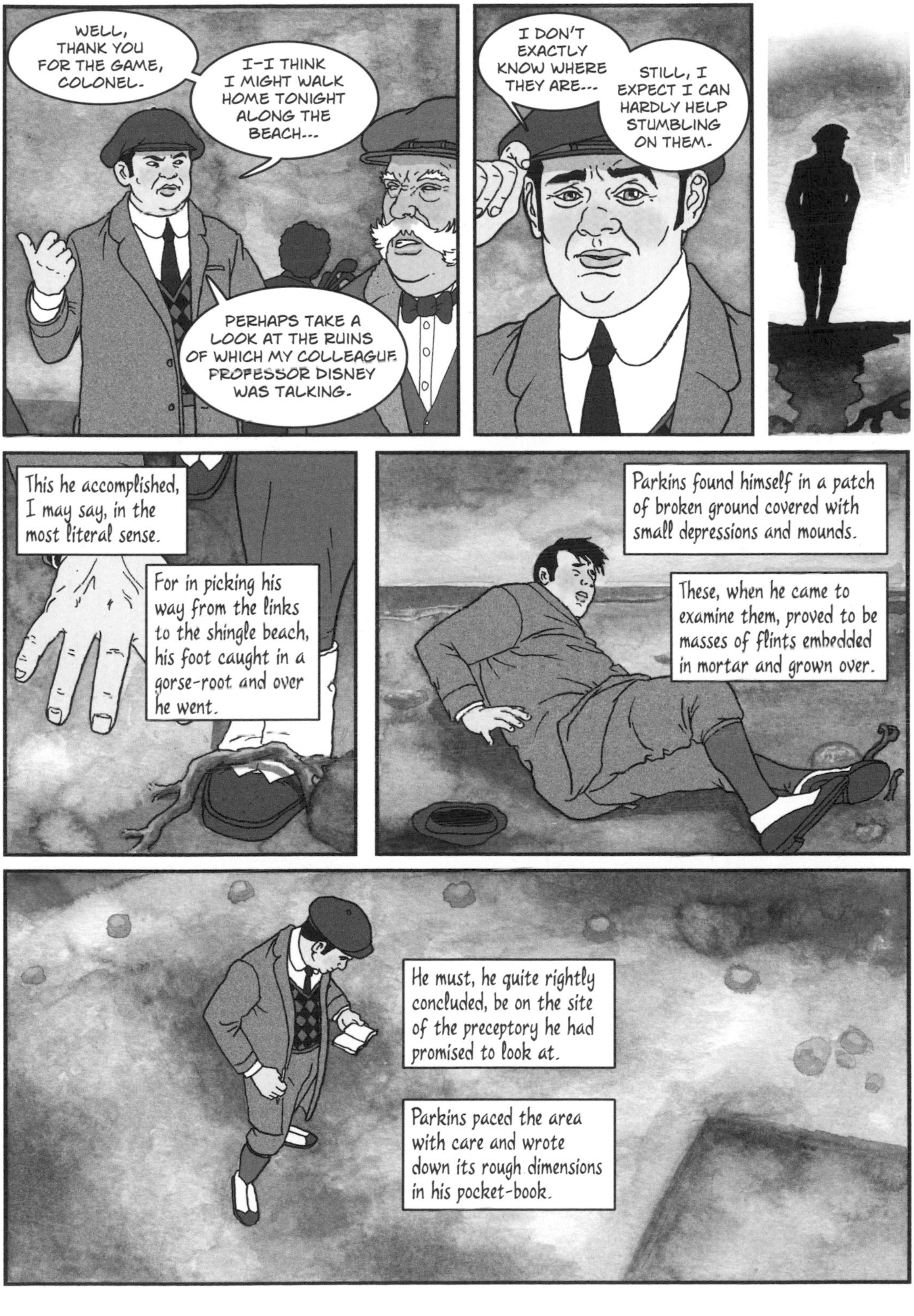
WELL, THANK YOU FOR THE GAME, COLONEL.
I-I THINK I MIGHT WALK HOME TONIGHT ALONG THE BEACH...
PERHAPS TAKE A LOOK AT THE RUINS OF WHICH MY COLLEAGUE PROFESSOR DISNEY WAS TALKING.
I DON'T EXACTLY KNOW WHERE THEY ARE...
STILL, I EXPECT I CAN HARDLY HELP STUMBLING ON THEM.
This he accomplished, I may say, in the most literal sense.
For in picking his way from the links to the shingle beach, his foot caught in a gorse-root and over he went.
Parkins found himself in a patch of broken ground covered with small depressions and mounds.
These, when he came to examine them, proved to be masses of flints embedded in mortar and grown over.
He must, he quite rightly concluded, be on the site of the preceptory he had promised to look at.
Parkins paced the area with care and wrote down its rough dimensions in his pocket-book.

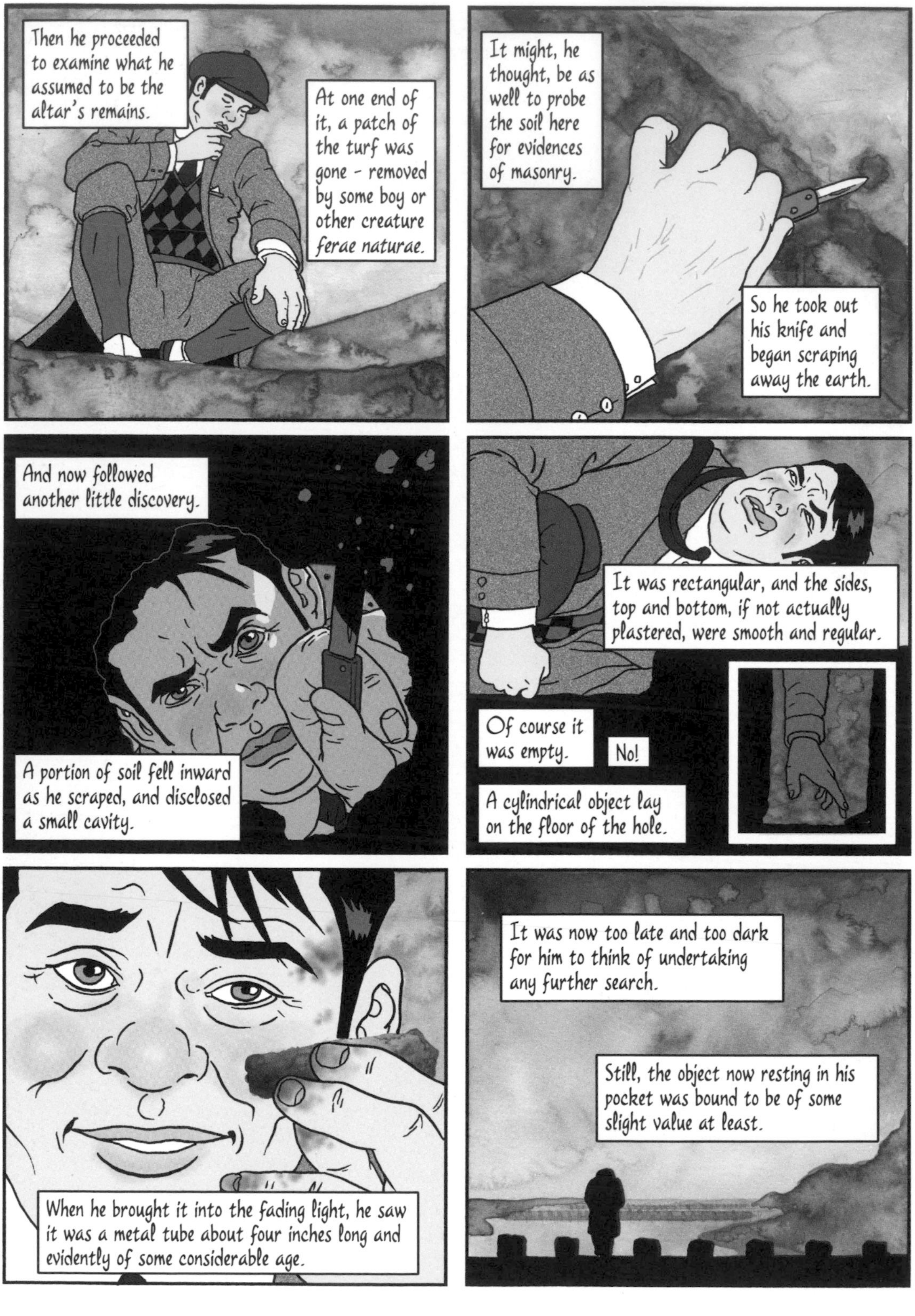
Then he proceeded to examine what he assumed to be the altar's remains.
At one end of it, a patch of the turf was gone - removed by some boy or other creature ferae naturae.
It might, he thought, be as well to probe the soil here for evidences of masonry.
So he took out his knife and began scraping away the earth.
And now followed another little discovery.
A portion of soil fell inward as he scraped, and disclosed a small cavity.
It was rectangular, and the sides, top and bottom, if not actually plastered, were smooth and regular.
Of course it was empty.
No!
A cylindrical object lay on the floor of the hole.
When he brought it into the fading light, he saw it was a metal tube about four inches long and evidently of some considerable age.
It was now too late and too dark for him to think of undertaking any further search.
Still, the object now resting in his pocket was bound to be of some slight value at least.

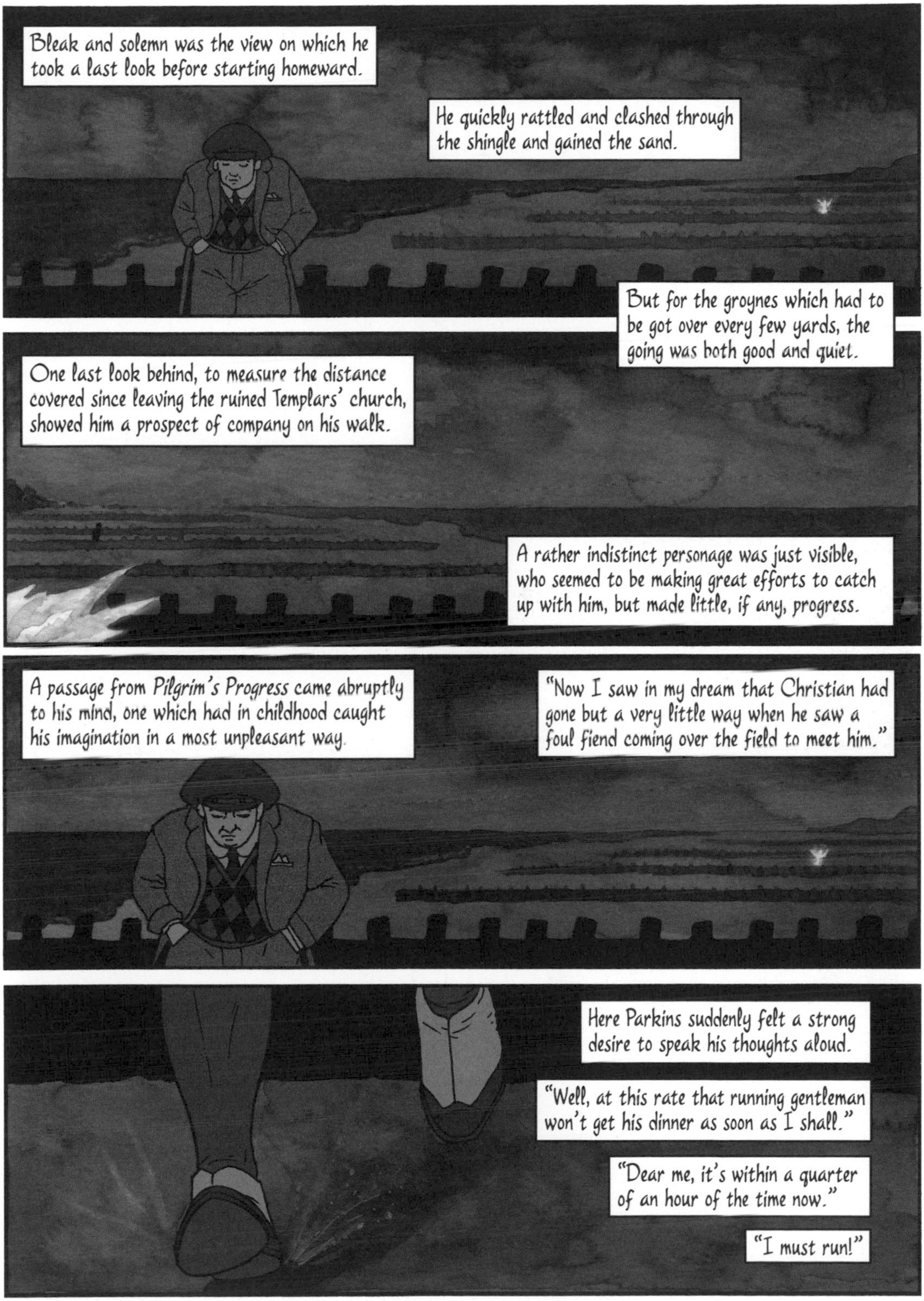
Bleak and solemn was the view on which he took a last look before starting homeward.
He quickly rattled and clashed through the shingle and gained the sand.
But for the groynes which had to be got over every few yards, the going was both good and quiet.
One last look behind, to measure the distance covered since leaving the ruined Templars' church, showed him a prospect of company on his walk.
A rather indistinct personage was just visible, who seemed to be making great efforts to catch up with him, but made little, if any, progress.
A passage from *Pilgrim's Progress* came abruptly to his mind, one which had in childhood caught his imagination in a most unpleasant way.
"Now I saw in my dream that Christian had gone but a very little way when he saw a foul fiend coming over the field to meet him."
Here Parkins suddenly felt a strong desire to speak his thoughts aloud.
"Well, at this rate that running gentleman won't get his dinner as soon as I shall."
"Dear me, it's within a quarter of an hour of the time now."
"I must run!"

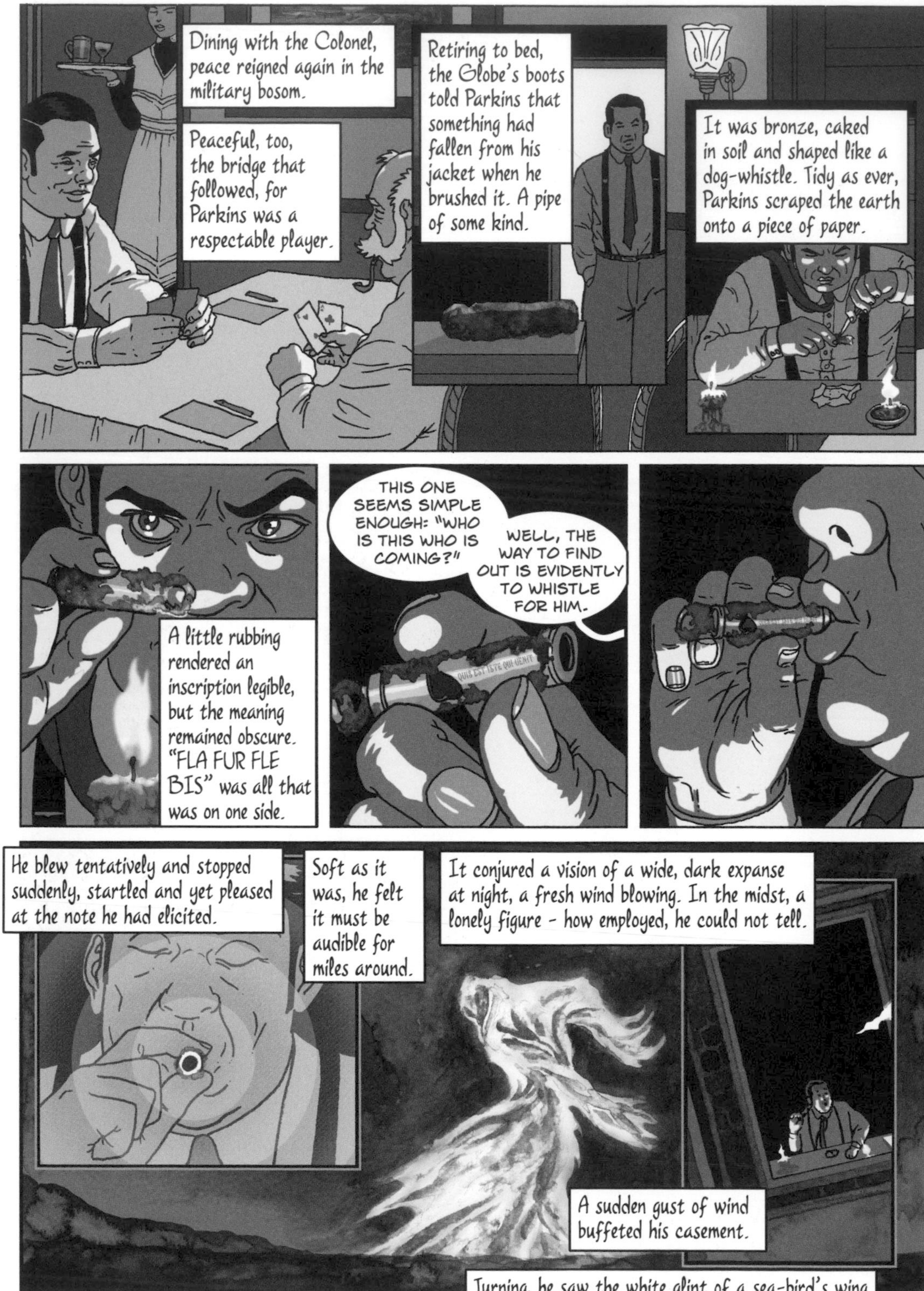
Dining with the Colonel, peace reigned again in the military bosom.
Peaceful, too, the bridge that followed, for Parkins was a respectable player.
Retiring to bed, the Globe's boots told Parkins that something had fallen from his jacket when he brushed it. A pipe of some kind.
It was bronze, caked in soil and shaped like a dog-whistle. Tidy as ever, Parkins scraped the earth onto a piece of paper.
A little rubbing rendered an inscription legible, but the meaning remained obscure. "FLA FUR FLE BIS" was all that was on one side.
THIS ONE SEEMS SIMPLE ENOUGH: "WHO IS THIS WHO IS COMING?"
WELL, THE WAY TO FIND OUT IS EVIDENTLY TO WHISTLE FOR HIM.
He blew tentatively and stopped suddenly, startled and yet pleased at the note he had elicited.
Soft as it was, he felt it must be audible for miles around.
It conjured a vision of a wide, dark expanse at night, a fresh wind blowing. In the midst, a lonely figure - how employed, he could not tell.
A sudden gust of wind buffeted his casement.
Turning, he saw the white glint of a sea-bird's wing somewhere outside the dark panes.

The sound of the whistle had so fascinated him that he could not help trying it once more, this time more boldly.

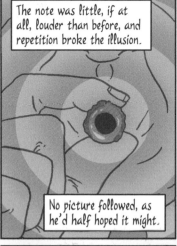

The note was little, if at all, louder than before, and repetition broke the illusion.

No picture followed, as he'd half hoped it might.

GOODNESS! WHAT FORCE THE WIND CAN GET UP IN A FEW MINUTES! WHAT A TREMENDOUS GUST!

I KNEW THAT WINDOW-FASTENING WAS NO USE!

AH! I THOUGHT SO – BOTH CANDLES OUT.

IT'S ENOUGH TO TEAR THE ROOM TO PIECES!

Struggling to close the small casement, he felt he were pushing back a sturdy burglar, so strong was the pressure.

Relighting his candle, Parkins looked to see what damage had been done.

Nothing seemed amiss. No window glass was even broken.

WELL, ALL THAT NOISE ROUSED ONE PERSON AT LEAST!

IT MUST BE THE COLONEL I CAN HEAR. STUMPING IN HIS STOCKINGED FEET ABOVE, AND GROWLING.

The wind moaned, sounding to Parkins so desolate that fanciful people might have felt quite uncomfortable.

Even the unimaginative might be happier without it.

He lay counting his heartbeats, convinced of some disorder. His only consolation was that a near neighbour was tossing and rustling in his bed, too.

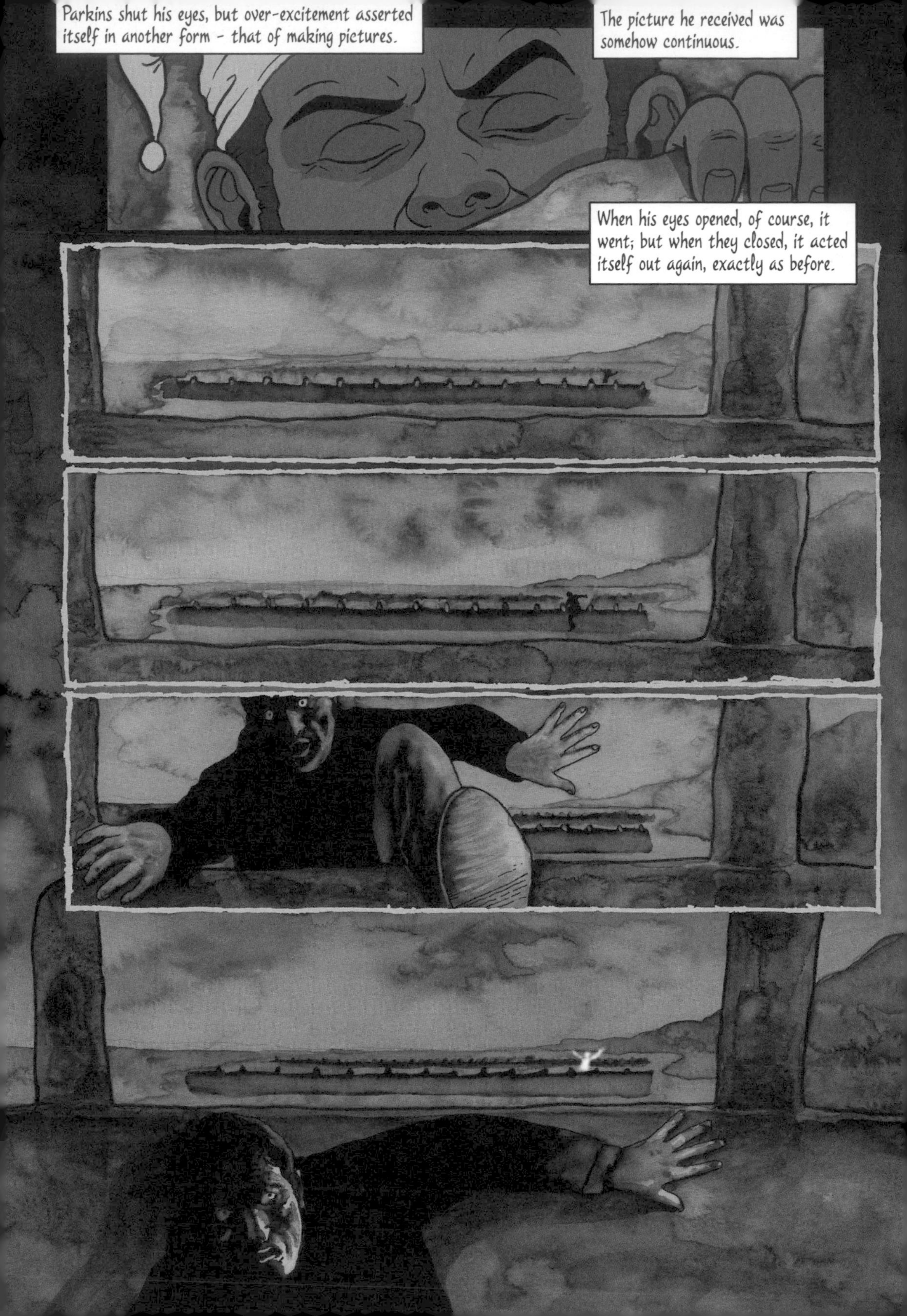
Parkins shut his eyes, but over-excitement asserted itself in another form - that of making pictures.
The picture he received was somehow continuous.
When his eyes opened, of course, it went; but when they closed, it acted itself out again, exactly as before.

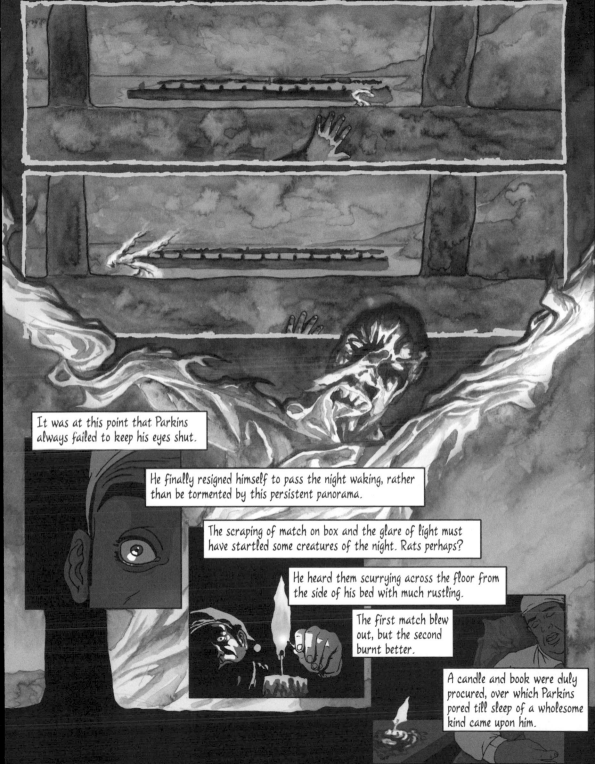

It was at this point that Parkins always failed to keep his eyes shut.

He finally resigned himself to pass the night waking, rather than be tormented by this persistent panorama.

The scraping of match on box and the glare of light must have startled some creatures of the night. Rats perhaps?

He heard them scurrying across the floor from the side of his bed with much rustling.

The first match blew out, but the second burnt better.

A candle and book were duly procured, over which Parkins pored till sleep of a wholesome kind came upon him.

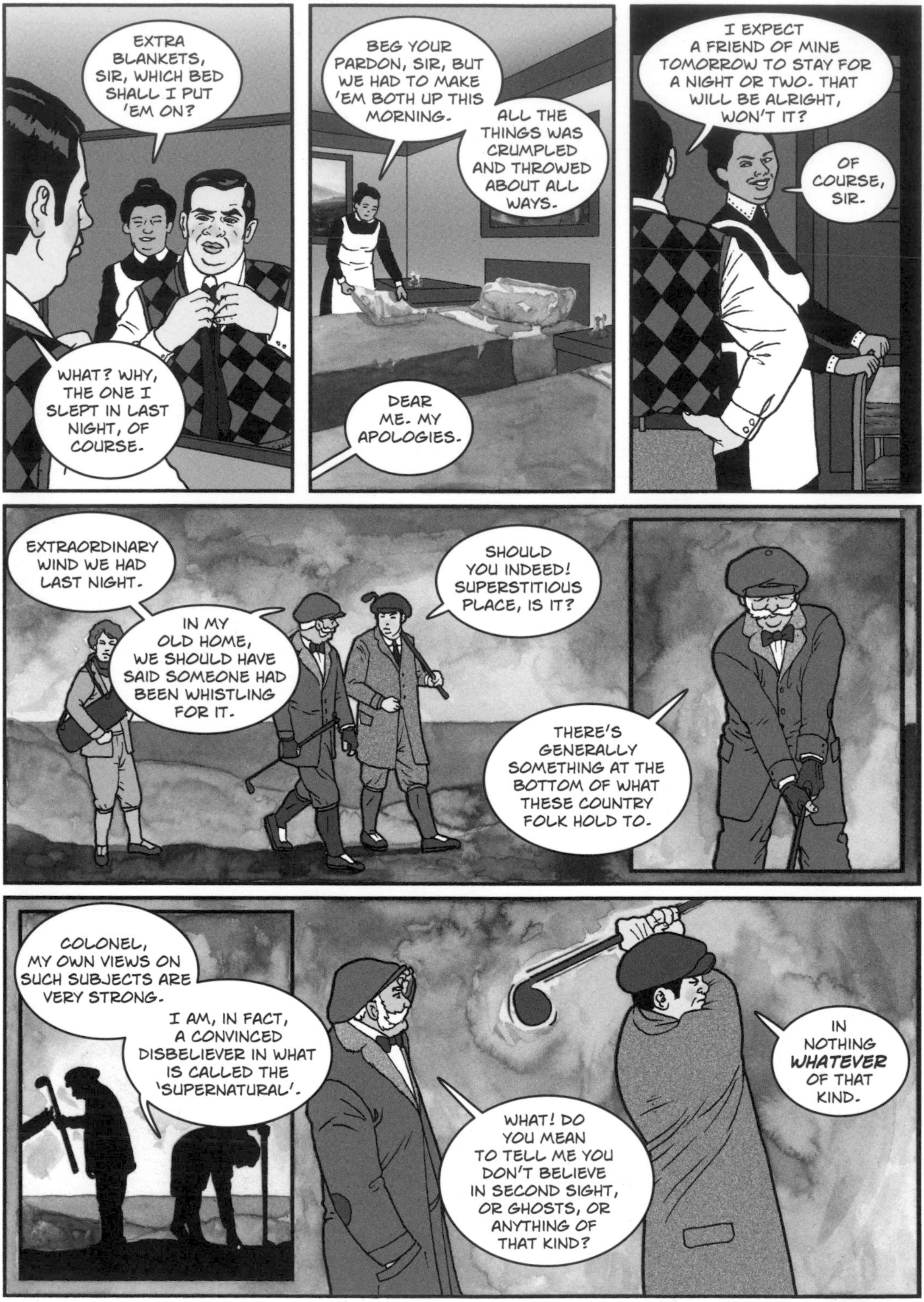
EXTRA BLANKETS, SIR, WHICH BED SHALL I PUT 'EM ON?
WHAT? WHY, THE ONE I SLEPT IN LAST NIGHT, OF COURSE.
BEG YOUR PARDON, SIR, BUT WE HAD TO MAKE 'EM BOTH UP THIS MORNING.
ALL THE THINGS WAS CRUMPLED AND THROWED ABOUT ALL WAYS.
DEAR ME. MY APOLOGIES.
I EXPECT A FRIEND OF MINE TOMORROW TO STAY FOR A NIGHT OR TWO. THAT WILL BE ALRIGHT, WON'T IT?
OF COURSE, SIR.
EXTRAORDINARY WIND WE HAD LAST NIGHT.
IN MY OLD HOME, WE SHOULD HAVE SAID SOMEONE HAD BEEN WHISTLING FOR IT.
SHOULD YOU INDEED! SUPERSTITIOUS PLACE, IS IT?
THERE'S GENERALLY SOMETHING AT THE BOTTOM OF WHAT THESE COUNTRY FOLK HOLD TO.
COLONEL, MY OWN VIEWS ON SUCH SUBJECTS ARE VERY STRONG.
I AM, IN FACT, A CONVINCED DISBELIEVER IN WHAT IS CALLED THE 'SUPERNATURAL'.
WHAT! DO YOU MEAN TO TELL ME YOU DON'T BELIEVE IN SECOND SIGHT, OR GHOSTS, OR ANYTHING OF THAT KIND?
IN NOTHING WHATEVER OF THAT KIND.

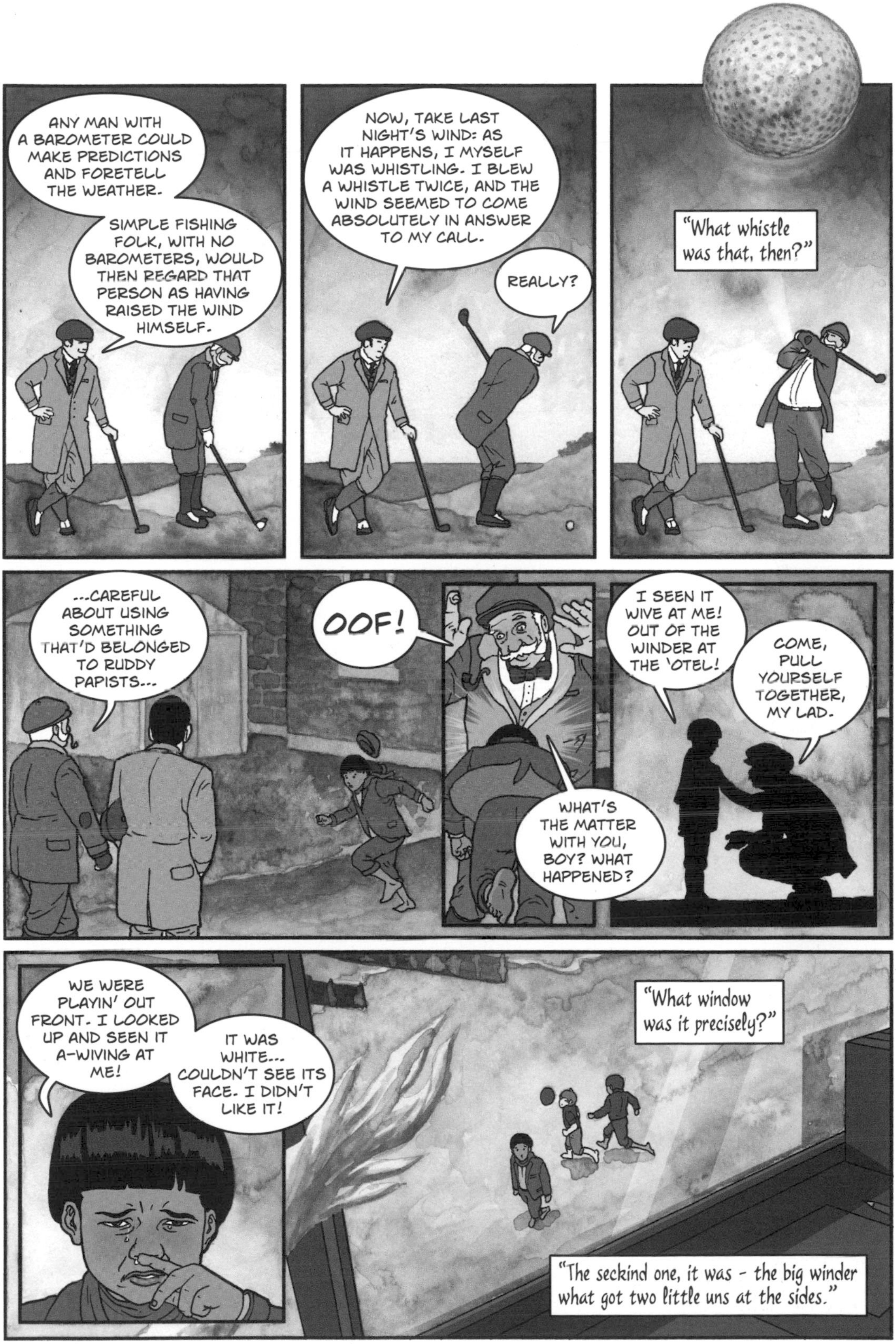
ANY MAN WITH A BAROMETER COULD MAKE PREDICTIONS AND FORETELL THE WEATHER.
SIMPLE FISHING FOLK, WITH NO BAROMETERS, WOULD THEN REGARD THAT PERSON AS HAVING RAISED THE WIND HIMSELF.
NOW, TAKE LAST NIGHT'S WIND: AS IT HAPPENS, I MYSELF WAS WHISTLING. I BLEW A WHISTLE TWICE, AND THE WIND SEEMED TO COME ABSOLUTELY IN ANSWER TO MY CALL.
REALLY?
"What whistle was that, then?"
...CAREFUL ABOUT USING SOMETHING THAT'D BELONGED TO RUDDY PAPISTS...
OOF!
WHAT'S THE MATTER WITH YOU, BOY? WHAT HAPPENED?
I SEEN IT WIVE AT ME! OUT OF THE WINDER AT THE 'OTEL!
COME, PULL YOURSELF TOGETHER, MY LAD.
WE WERE PLAYIN' OUT FRONT. I LOOKED UP AND SEEN IT A-WIVING AT ME!
IT WAS WHITE... COULDN'T SEE ITS FACE. I DIDN'T LIKE IT!
"What window was it precisely?"
"The seckind one, it was - the big winder what got two little uns at the sides."

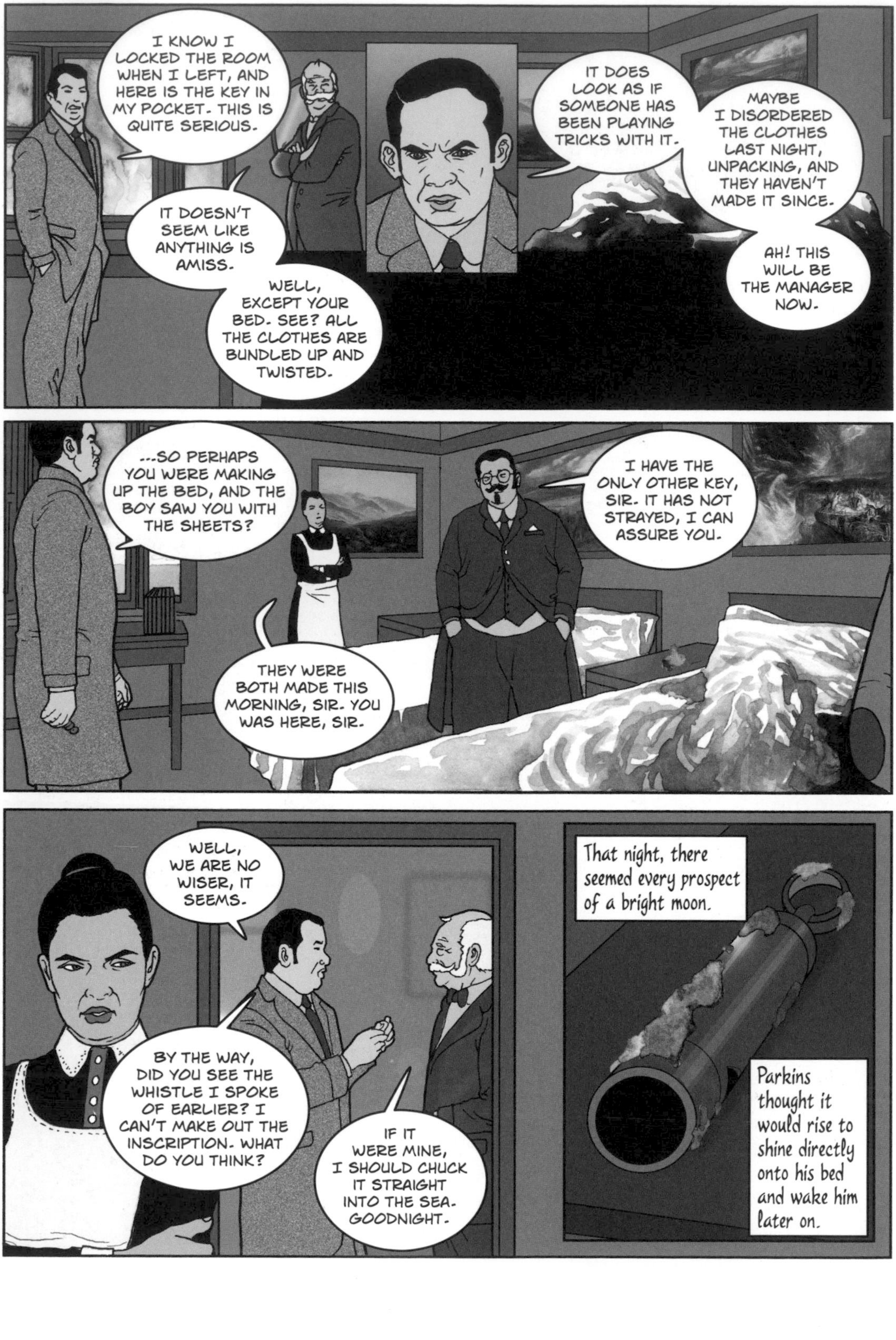
I KNOW I LOCKED THE ROOM WHEN I LEFT, AND HERE IS THE KEY IN MY POCKET. THIS IS QUITE SERIOUS.
IT DOESN'T SEEM LIKE ANYTHING IS AMISS.
WELL, EXCEPT YOUR BED. SEE? ALL THE CLOTHES ARE BUNDLED UP AND TWISTED.
IT DOES LOOK AS IF SOMEONE HAS BEEN PLAYING TRICKS WITH IT.
MAYBE I DISORDERED THE CLOTHES LAST NIGHT, UNPACKING, AND THEY HAVEN'T MADE IT SINCE.
AH! THIS WILL BE THE MANAGER NOW.
...SO PERHAPS YOU WERE MAKING UP THE BED, AND THE BOY SAW YOU WITH THE SHEETS?
THEY WERE BOTH MADE THIS MORNING, SIR. YOU WAS HERE, SIR.
I HAVE THE ONLY OTHER KEY, SIR. IT HAS NOT STRAYED, I CAN ASSURE YOU.
WELL, WE ARE NO WISER, IT SEEMS.
BY THE WAY, DID YOU SEE THE WHISTLE I SPOKE OF EARLIER? I CAN'T MAKE OUT THE INSCRIPTION. WHAT DO YOU THINK?
IF IT WERE MINE, I SHOULD CHUCK IT STRAIGHT INTO THE SEA. GOODNIGHT.
That night, there seemed every prospect of a bright moon.
Parkins thought it would rise to shine directly onto his bed and wake him later on.

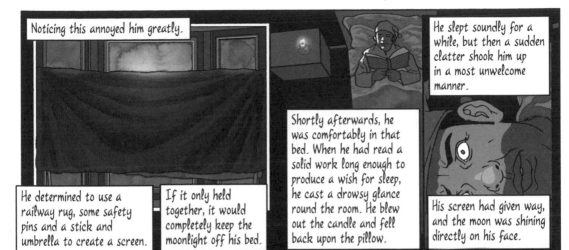

Noticing this annoyed him greatly.

He slept soundly for a while, but then a sudden clatter shook him up in a most unwelcome manner.

Shortly afterwards, he was comfortably in that bed. When he had read a solid work long enough to produce a wish for sleep, he cast a drowsy glance round the room. He blew out the candle and fell back upon the pillow.

His screen had given way, and the moon was shining directly on his face.

He determined to use a railway rug, some safety pins and a stick and umbrella to create a screen.

If it only held together, it would completely keep the moonlight off his bed.

This was highly irritating. Could he get up and reconstruct the screen? Or could he sleep if he did not?

What was that? A movement. In the empty bed on the opposite side of the room.

Rats maybe, rustling the bedsheets...?

I have in a dream thirty years back seen the same thing happen.

The reader, however, will hardly imagine how dreadful it was to him, to see a figure suddenly sit up...

...in what he had known was an empty bed.

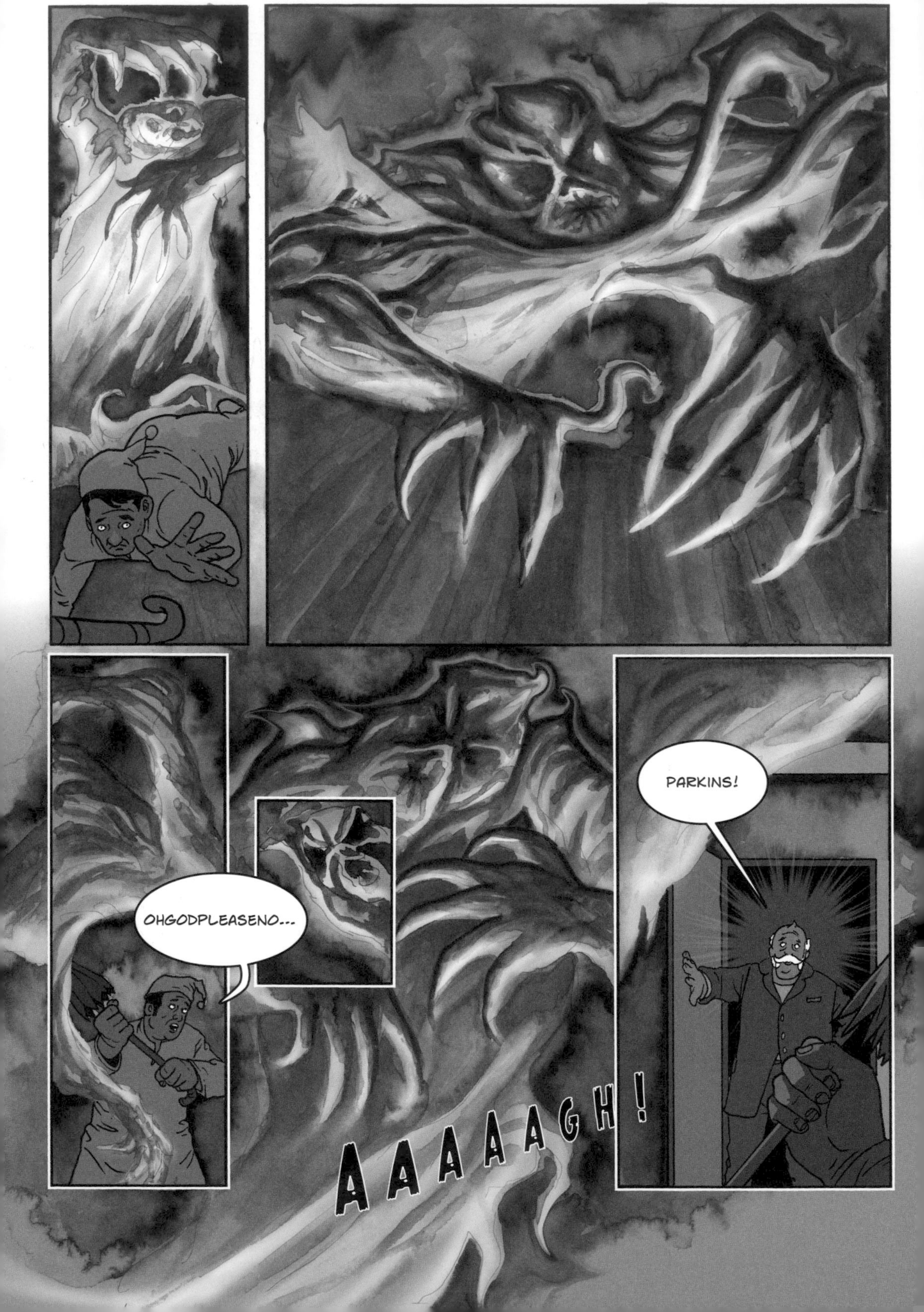
OHGODPLEASENO...
PARKINS!
AAAAAGH!

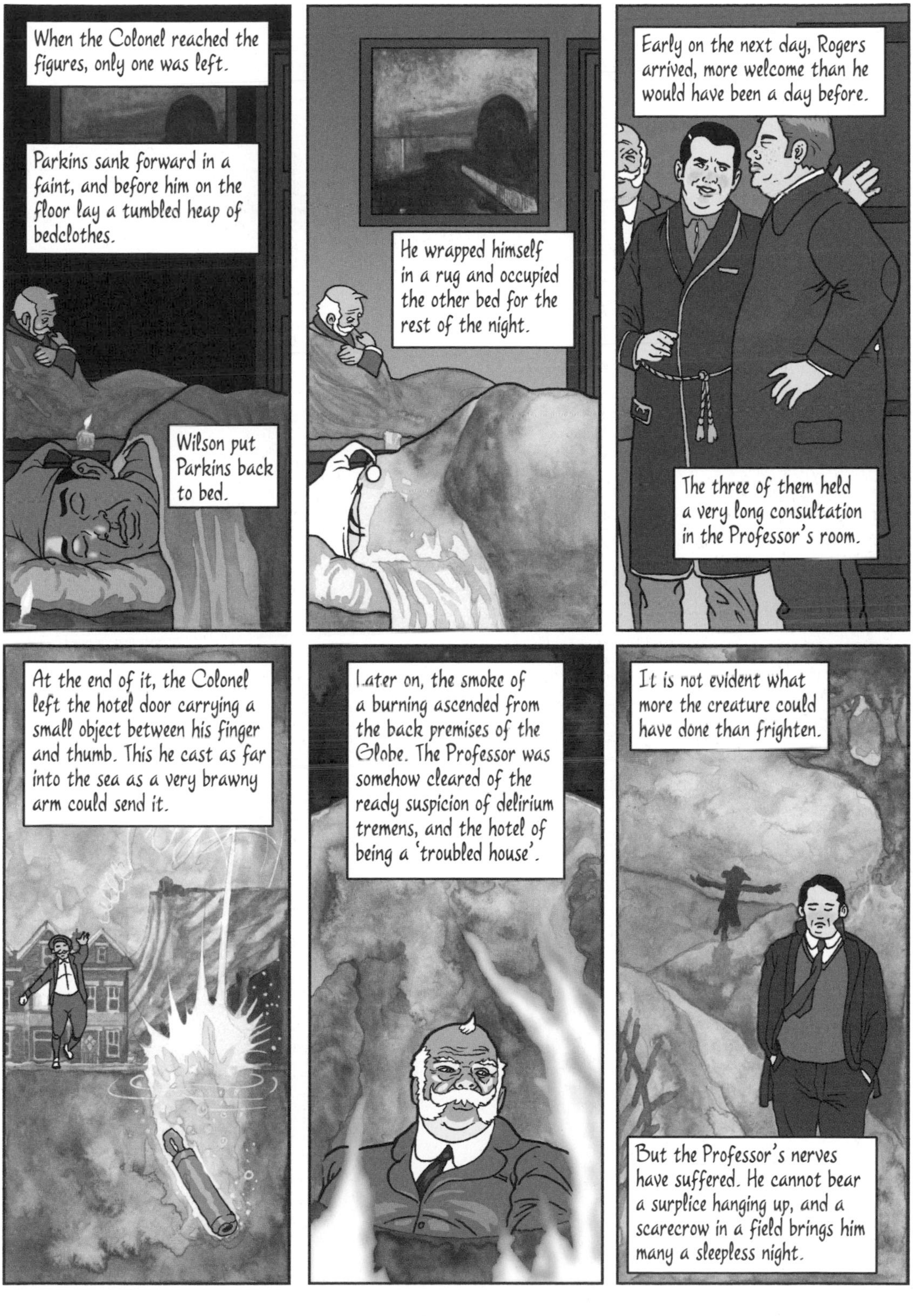
When the Colonel reached the figures, only one was left.
Parkins sank forward in a faint, and before him on the floor lay a tumbled heap of bedclothes.
Wilson put Parkins back to bed.
He wrapped himself in a rug and occupied the other bed for the rest of the night.
Early on the next day, Rogers arrived, more welcome than he would have been a day before.
The three of them held a very long consultation in the Professor's room.
At the end of it, the Colonel left the hotel door carrying a small object between his finger and thumb. This he cast as far into the sea as a very brawny arm could send it.
Later on, the smoke of a burning ascended from the back premises of the Globe. The Professor was somehow cleared of the ready suspicion of delirium tremens, and the hotel of being a 'troubled house'.
It is not evident what more the creature could have done than frighten.
But the Professor's nerves have suffered. He cannot bear a surplice hanging up, and a scarecrow in a field brings him many a sleepless night.

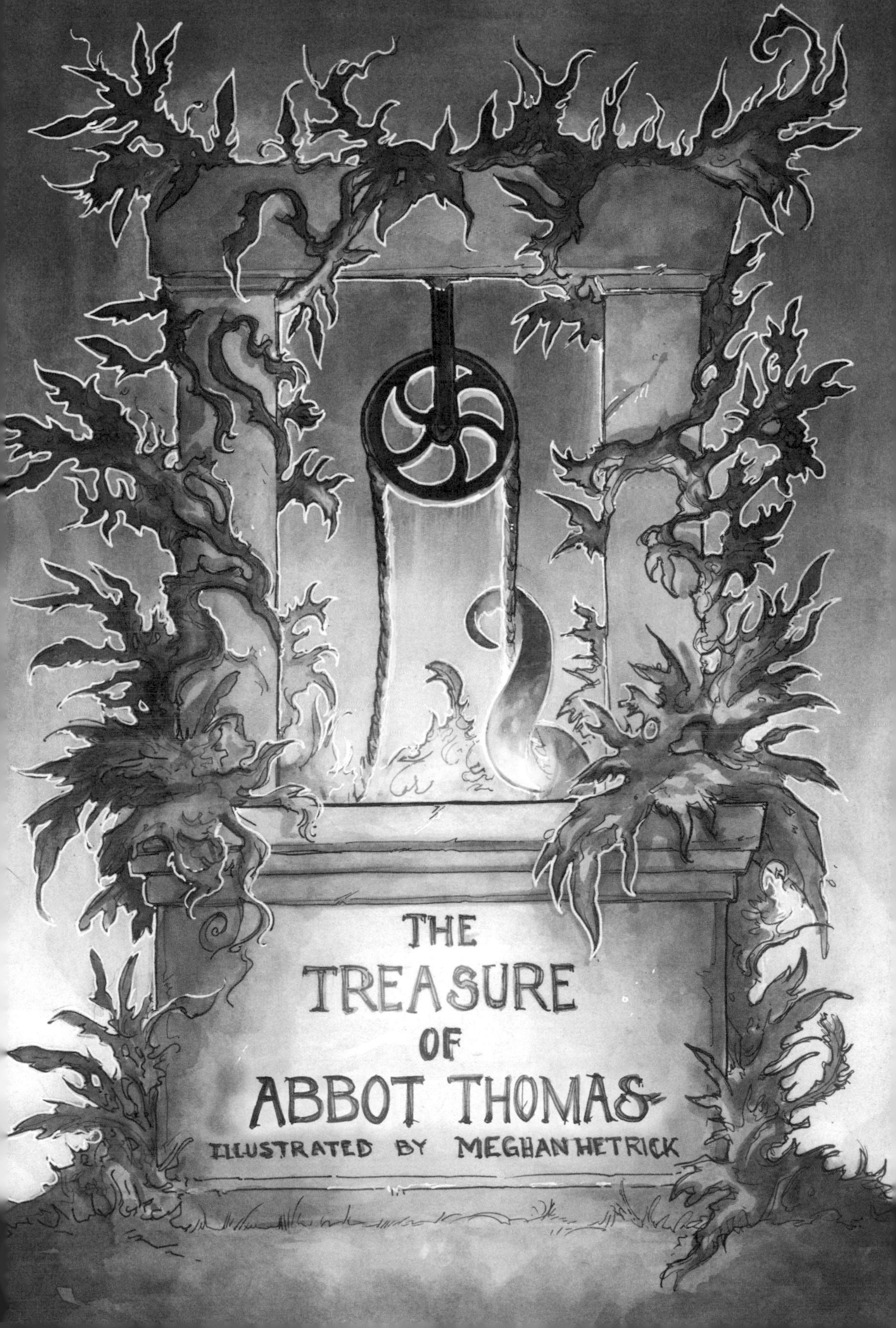
THE
TREASURE
OF
ABBOT THOMAS
ILLUSTRATED BY MEGHAN HETRICK

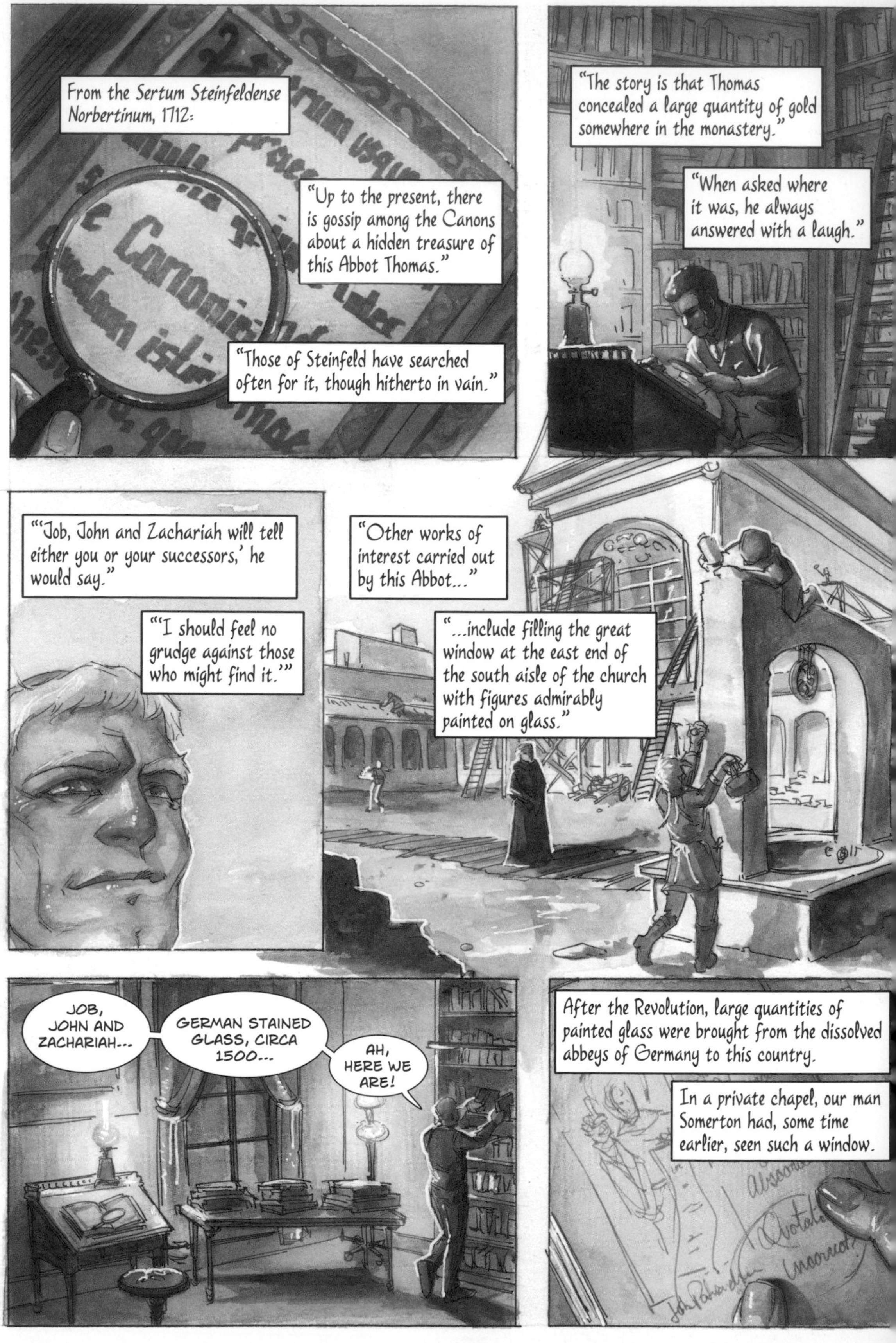
From the Sertum Steinfeldense Norbertinum, 1712:
"Up to the present, there is gossip among the Canons about a hidden treasure of this Abbot Thomas."
"Those of Steinfeld have searched often for it, though hitherto in vain."
"The story is that Thomas concealed a large quantity of gold somewhere in the monastery."
"When asked where it was, he always answered with a laugh."
"'Job, John and Zachariah will tell either you or your successors,' he would say."
"'I should feel no grudge against those who might find it.'"
"Other works of interest carried out by this Abbot..."
"...include filling the great window at the east end of the south aisle of the church with figures admirably painted on glass."
JOB, JOHN AND ZACHARIAH...
GERMAN STAINED GLASS, CIRCA 1500...
AH, HERE WE ARE!
After the Revolution, large quantities of painted glass were brought from the dissolved abbeys of Germany to this country.
In a private chapel, our man Somerton had, some time earlier, seen such a window.

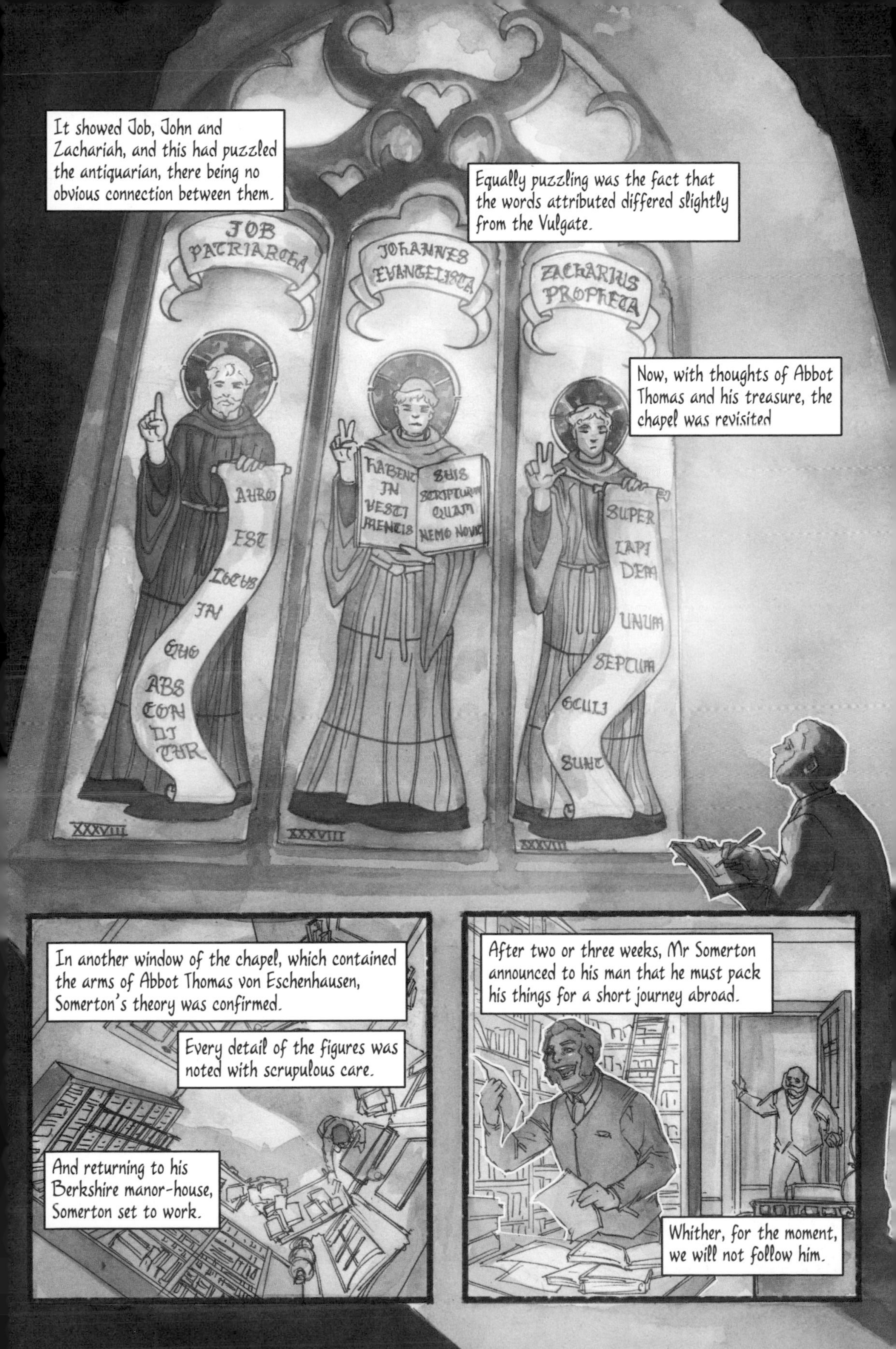
It showed Job, John and Zachariah, and this had puzzled the antiquarian, there being no obvious connection between them.
Equally puzzling was the fact that the words attributed differed slightly from the Vulgate.
JOB PATRIARCHA
JOHANNES EVANGELISTA
ZACHARIUS PROPHETA
Now, with thoughts of Abbot Thomas and his treasure, the chapel was revisited
In another window of the chapel, which contained the arms of Abbot Thomas von Eschenhausen, Somerton's theory was confirmed.
Every detail of the figures was noted with scrupulous care.
And returning to his Berkshire manor-house, Somerton set to work.
After two or three weeks, Mr Somerton announced to his man that he must pack his things for a short journey abroad.
Whither, for the moment, we will not follow him.

Mr Gregory, the Rector of Parsbury, had strolled out before breakfast, with intent to meet the postman and sniff the cool air.

Honourd Sir, I am in a great anxeity about Master.

I wish to Beg you Sir if you could be so good as Step over.

He Has add a Nastey Shock and keeps His Bedd.

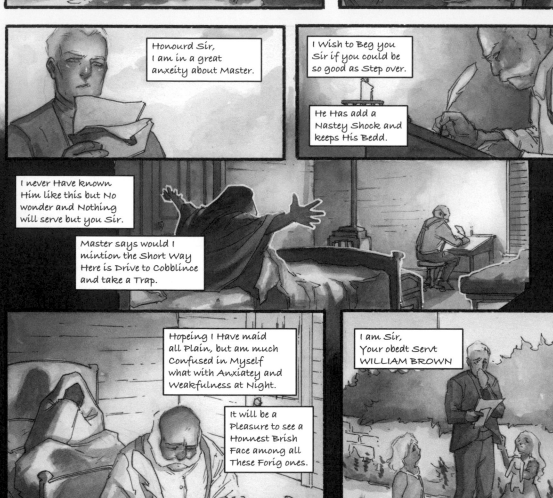

I never Have known Him like this but No wonder and Nothing will serve but you Sir.

Master says would I mintion the Short Way Here is Drive to Cobblince and take a Trap.

Hopeing I Have maid all Plain, but am much Confused in Myself what with Anxiatey and Weakfulness at Night.

It will be a Pleasure to see a Honnest Brish Face among all These Forig ones.

I am Sir, Your obedt Servt WILLIAM BROWN

P.S. – The Villiage for Town I will not Turm It is name Steenfeld.

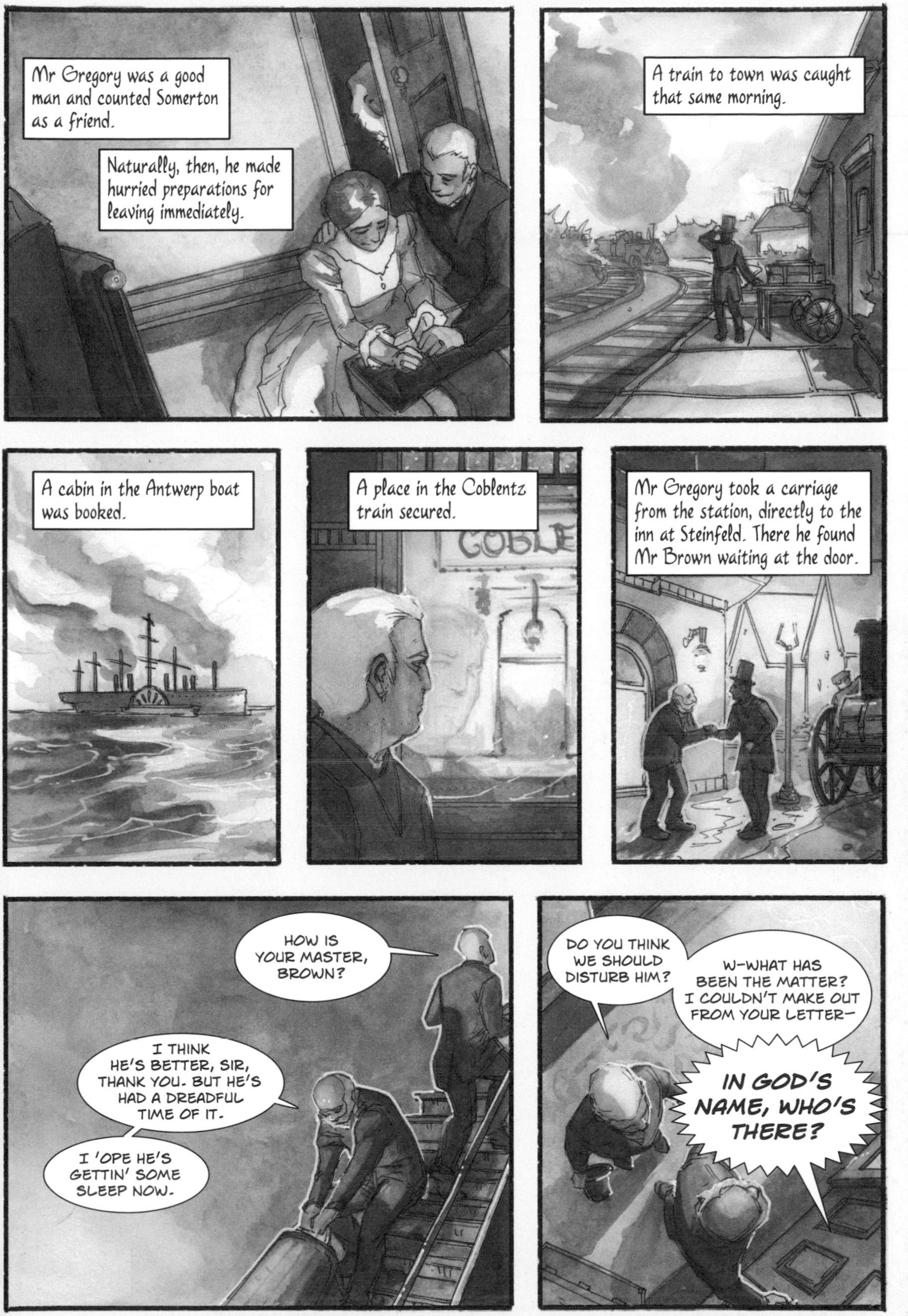

Mr Gregory was a good man and counted Somerton as a friend.
Naturally, then, he made hurried preparations for leaving immediately.
A train to town was caught that same morning.
A cabin in the Antwerp boat was booked.
A place in the Coblentz train secured.
COBLE
Mr Gregory took a carriage from the station, directly to the inn at Steinfeld. There he found Mr Brown waiting at the door.
HOW IS YOUR MASTER, BROWN?
I THINK HE'S BETTER, SIR, THANK YOU. BUT HE'S HAD A DREADFUL TIME OF IT.
I 'OPE HE'S GETTIN' SOME SLEEP NOW.
DO YOU THINK WE SHOULD DISTURB HIM?
W-WHAT HAS BEEN THE MATTER? I COULDN'T MAKE OUT FROM YOUR LETTER–
IN GOD'S NAME, WHO'S THERE?

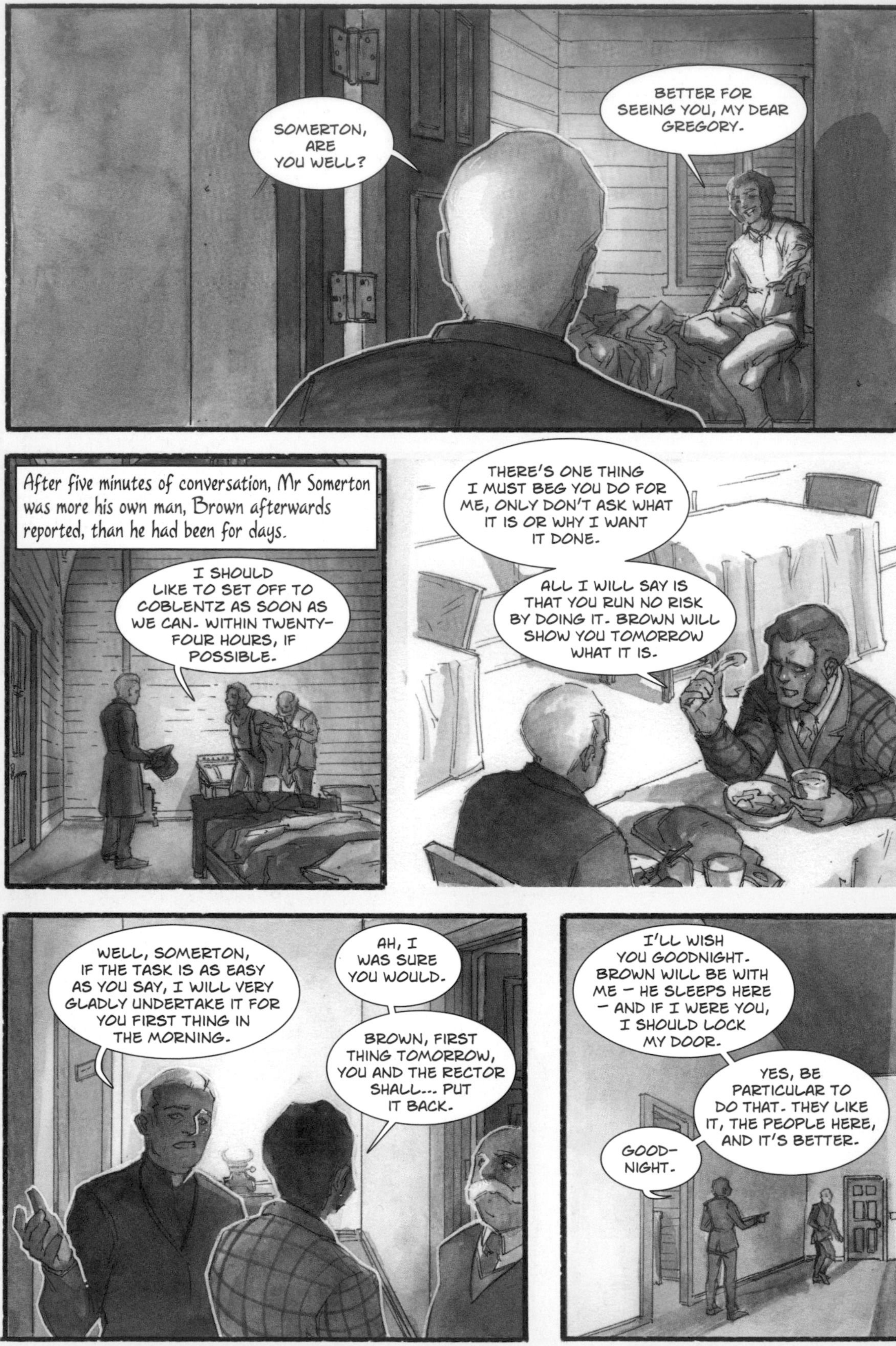
SOMERTON, ARE YOU WELL?
BETTER FOR SEEING YOU, MY DEAR GREGORY.
After five minutes of conversation, Mr Somerton was more his own man, Brown afterwards reported, than he had been for days.
I SHOULD LIKE TO SET OFF TO COBLENTZ AS SOON AS WE CAN. WITHIN TWENTY-FOUR HOURS, IF POSSIBLE.
THERE'S ONE THING I MUST BEG YOU DO FOR ME, ONLY DON'T ASK WHAT IT IS OR WHY I WANT IT DONE.
ALL I WILL SAY IS THAT YOU RUN NO RISK BY DOING IT. BROWN WILL SHOW YOU TOMORROW WHAT IT IS.
WELL, SOMERTON, IF THE TASK IS AS EASY AS YOU SAY, I WILL VERY GLADLY UNDERTAKE IT FOR YOU FIRST THING IN THE MORNING.
AH, I WAS SURE YOU WOULD.
BROWN, FIRST THING TOMORROW, YOU AND THE RECTOR SHALL... PUT IT BACK.
I'LL WISH YOU GOODNIGHT. BROWN WILL BE WITH ME — HE SLEEPS HERE — AND IF I WERE YOU, I SHOULD LOCK MY DOOR.
YES, BE PARTICULAR TO DO THAT. THEY LIKE IT, THE PEOPLE HERE, AND IT'S BETTER.
GOOD-NIGHT.

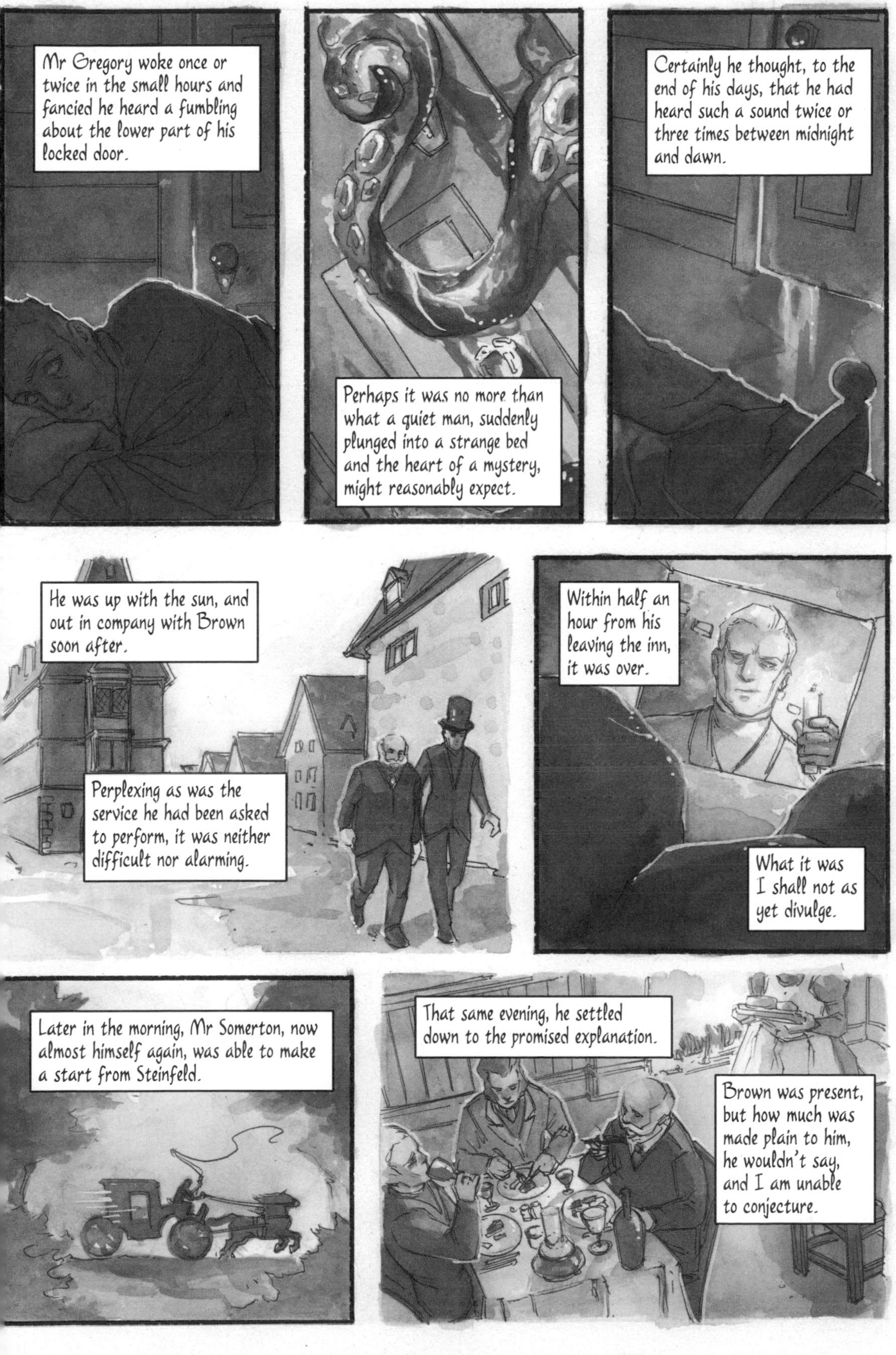
Mr Gregory woke once or twice in the small hours and fancied he heard a fumbling about the lower part of his locked door.
Perhaps it was no more than what a quiet man, suddenly plunged into a strange bed and the heart of a mystery, might reasonably expect.
Certainly he thought, to the end of his days, that he had heard such a sound twice or three times between midnight and dawn.
He was up with the sun, and out in company with Brown soon after.
Perplexing as was the service he had been asked to perform, it was neither difficult nor alarming.
Within half an hour from his leaving the inn, it was over.
What it was I shall not as yet divulge.
Later in the morning, Mr Somerton, now almost himself again, was able to make a start from Steinfeld.
That same evening, he settled down to the promised explanation.
Brown was present, but how much was made plain to him, he wouldn't say, and I am unable to conjecture.

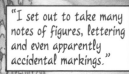

"My expedition had the object of tracing a connection with some old painted glass in Lord D–'s private chapel."

"I set out to take many notes of figures, lettering and even apparently accidental markings."

"The first task was the inscribed scrolls. I could not doubt that the first of these, that of Job, referred to the Abbot's treasure:"

"'There is a place for the gold where it is hidden.'"

"The scroll of St John was cryptic: 'They have on their vestures a writing which no man knoweth'."

"The robes had no inscriptions, just an ugly black border."

"But for astonishing luck, I'd have failed then."

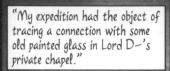

"The glass was incredibly dusty, and Lord D– happened to come in and see my blackened hands."

"He kindly insisted on sending for a Turk's-head broom to clean down the window."

"There must've been a rough piece in the broom, as I saw it had left a scratch and revealed yellow stain."

"I stopped the man in his work, and ran up to examine the place."

"What had come away was a thick black pigment. I found under this pigment two or three clearly formed capital letters in yellow stain on a clear ground."

"Of course, I could hardly contain my delight."

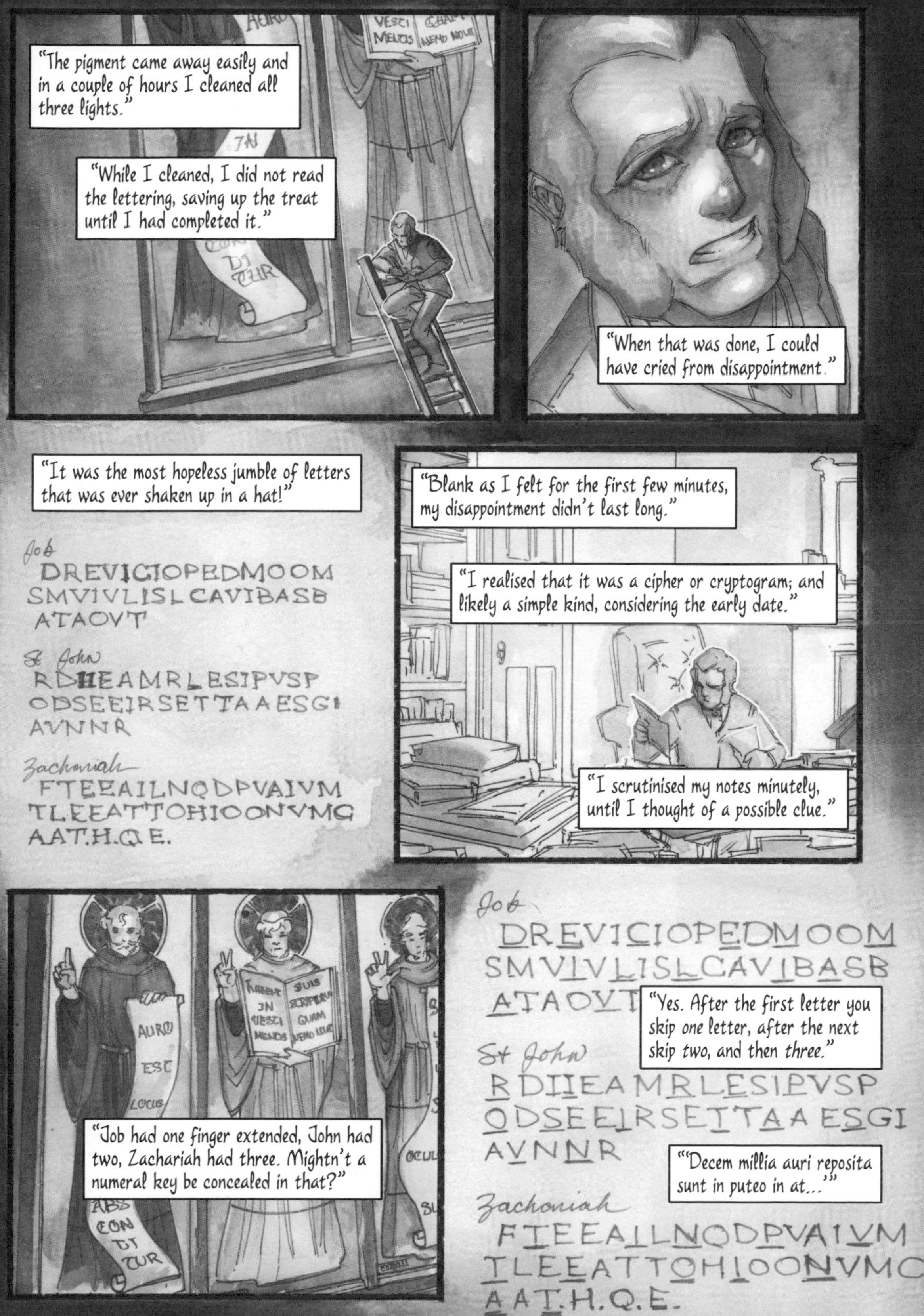
"The pigment came away easily and in a couple of hours I cleaned all three lights."
"While I cleaned, I did not read the lettering, saving up the treat until I had completed it."
"When that was done, I could have cried from disappointment."
"It was the most hopeless jumble of letters that was ever shaken up in a hat!"
Job
DREVICIOPEDMOOM
SMVIVLISLCAVIBASB
ATAOVT
St John
RDIIEAMRLESIPVSP
ODSEEIRSETTAAESGI
AVNNR
Zachariah
FTEEAILNQDPVAIVM
TLEEATTOHIOONVMG
AAT.H.Q.E.
"Blank as I felt for the first few minutes, my disappointment didn't last long."
"I realised that it was a cipher or cryptogram; and likely a simple kind, considering the early date."
"I scrutinised my notes minutely, until I thought of a possible clue."
AURO
EST
LOCUS
ABS
CON
DI
TUR
"Job had one finger extended, John had two, Zachariah had three. Mightn't a numeral key be concealed in that?"
Job
DREVICIOPEDMOOM
SMVIVLISLCAVIBASB
ATAOVT
"Yes. After the first letter you skip one letter, after the next skip two, and then three."
St John
RDIIEAMRLESIPVSP
ODSEEIRSETTAAESGI
AVNNR
"Decem millia auri reposita sunt in puteo in at..."
Zachoriah
FTEEAILNQDPVAIVM
TLEEATTOHIOONVMC
AAT.H.Q.E.

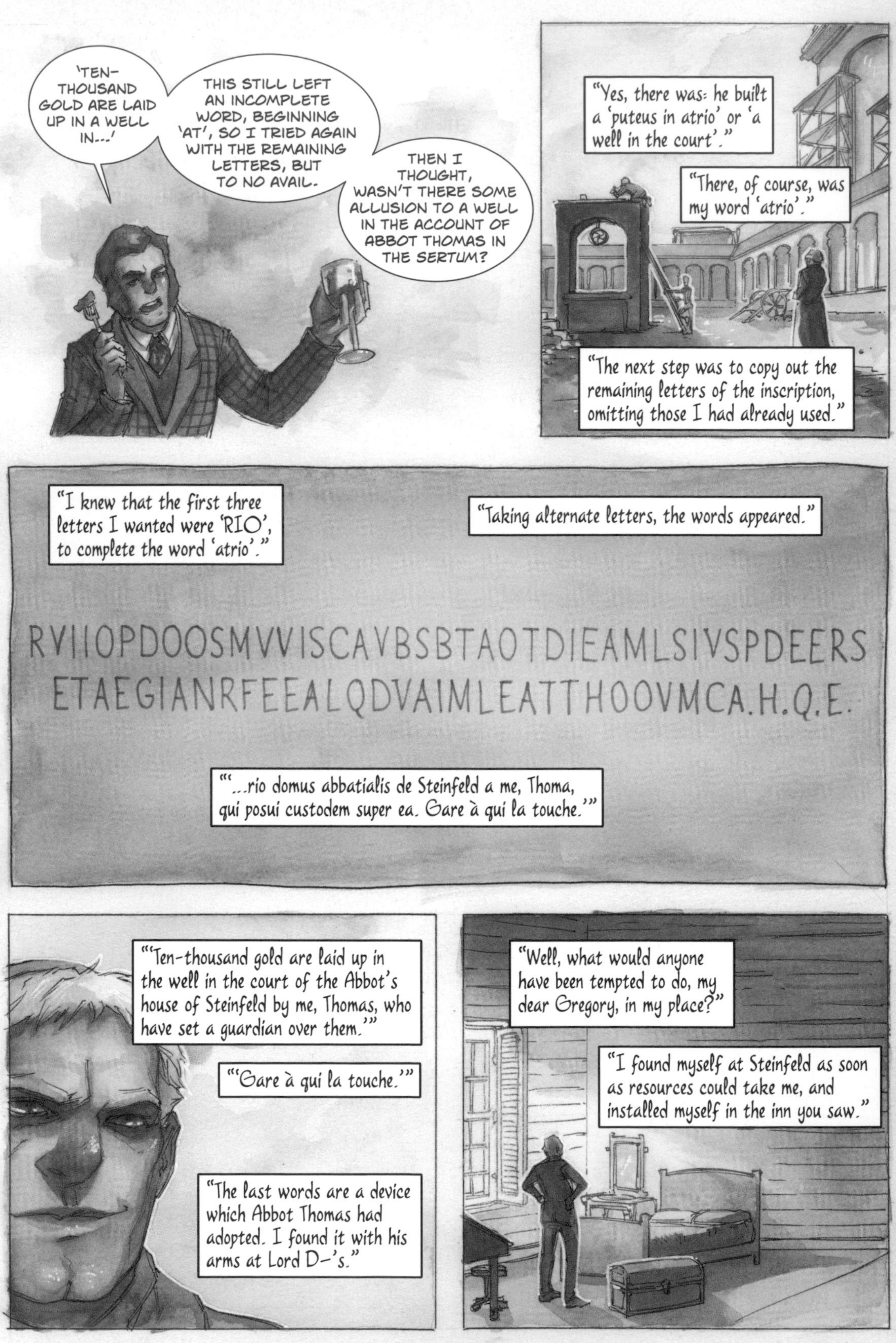

'TEN-THOUSAND GOLD ARE LAID UP IN A WELL IN...'
THIS STILL LEFT AN INCOMPLETE WORD, BEGINNING 'AT', SO I TRIED AGAIN WITH THE REMAINING LETTERS, BUT TO NO AVAIL.
THEN I THOUGHT, WASN'T THERE SOME ALLUSION TO A WELL IN THE ACCOUNT OF ABBOT THOMAS IN THE SERTUM?
"Yes, there was: he built a 'puteus in atrio' or 'a well in the court'."
"There, of course, was my word 'atrio'."
"The next step was to copy out the remaining letters of the inscription, omitting those I had already used."
"I knew that the first three letters I wanted were 'RIO', to complete the word 'atrio'."
"Taking alternate letters, the words appeared."
RVIIOPDOOSMVVISCAVBSBTAOTDIEAMLSIVSPDEERS
ETAEGIANRFEEALQDVAIMLEATTHOOVMCA.H.Q.E.
"'...rio domus abbatialis de Steinfeld a me, Thoma, qui posui custodem super ea. Gare à qui la touche.'"
"'Ten-thousand gold are laid up in the well in the court of the Abbot's house of Steinfeld by me, Thomas, who have set a guardian over them.'"
"'Gare à qui la touche.'"
"The last words are a device which Abbot Thomas had adopted. I found it with his arms at Lord D–'s."
"Well, what would anyone have been tempted to do, my dear Gregory, in my place?"
"I found myself at Steinfeld as soon as resources could take me, and installed myself in the inn you saw."

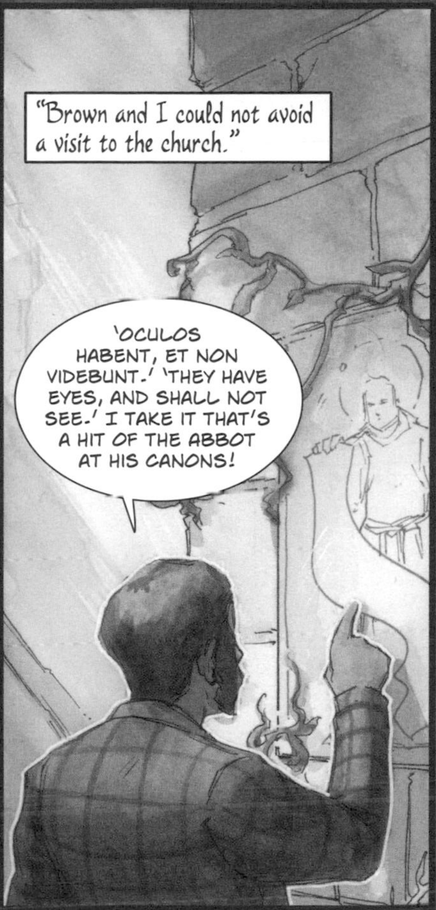
"Brown and I could not avoid a visit to the church."
'OCULOS HABENT, ET NON VIDEBUNT.' 'THEY HAVE EYES, AND SHALL NOT SEE.' I TAKE IT THAT'S A HIT OF THE ABBOT AT HIS CANONS!

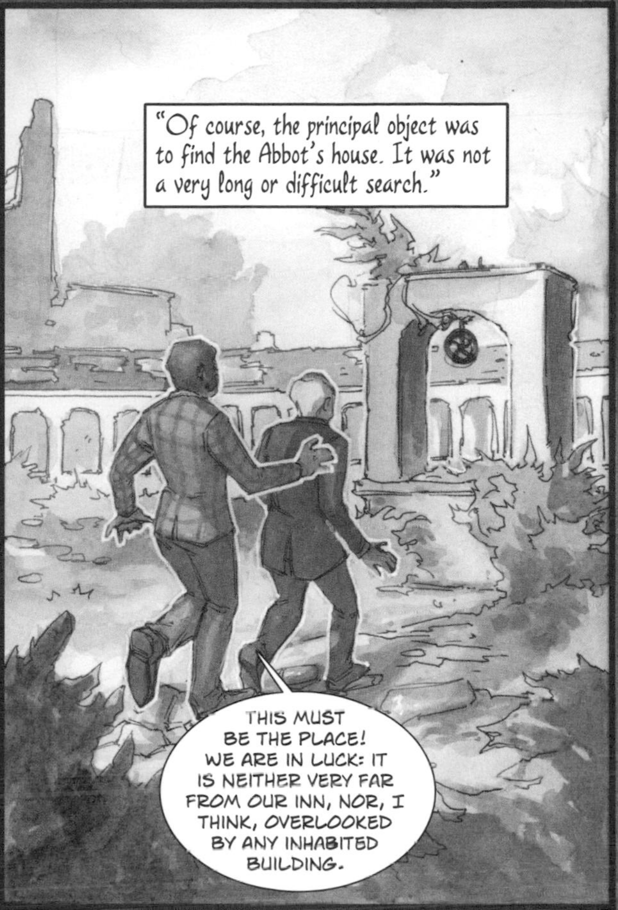
"Of course, the principal object was to find the Abbot's house. It was not a very long or difficult search."
THIS MUST BE THE PLACE! WE ARE IN LUCK: IT IS NEITHER VERY FAR FROM OUR INN, NOR, I THINK, OVERLOOKED BY ANY INHABITED BUILDING.

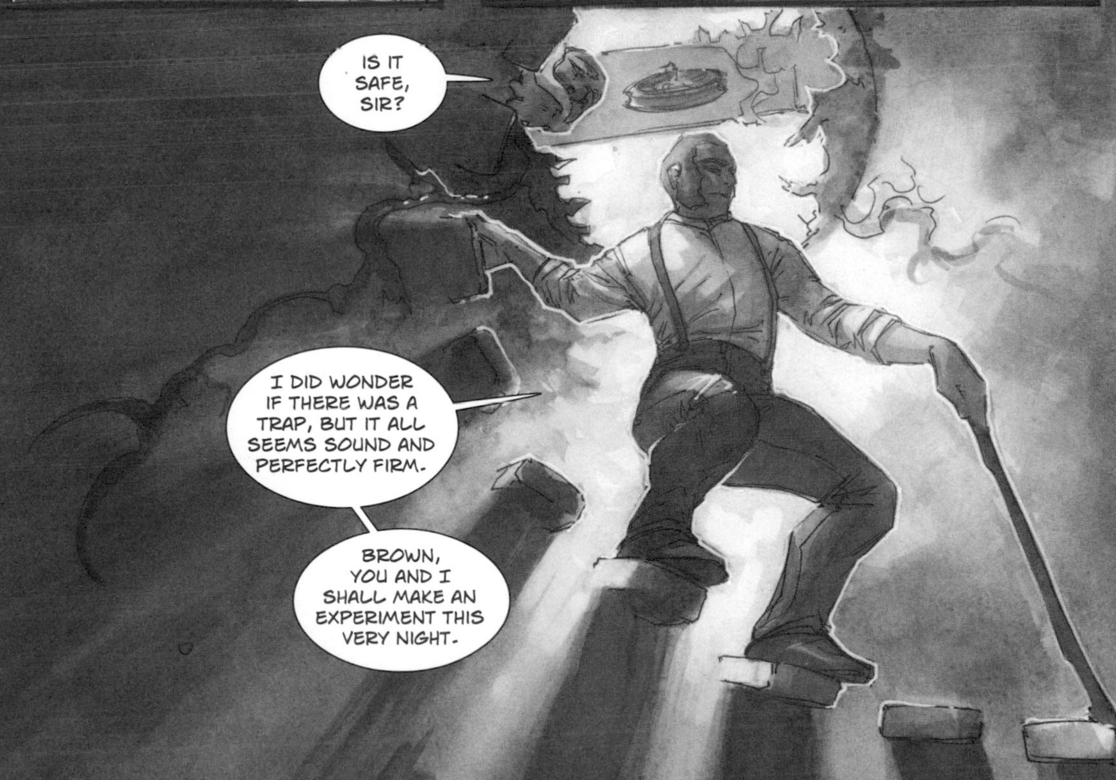
IS IT SAFE, SIR?
I DID WONDER IF THERE WAS A TRAP, BUT IT ALL SEEMS SOUND AND PERFECTLY FIRM.
BROWN, YOU AND I SHALL MAKE AN EXPERIMENT THIS VERY NIGHT.

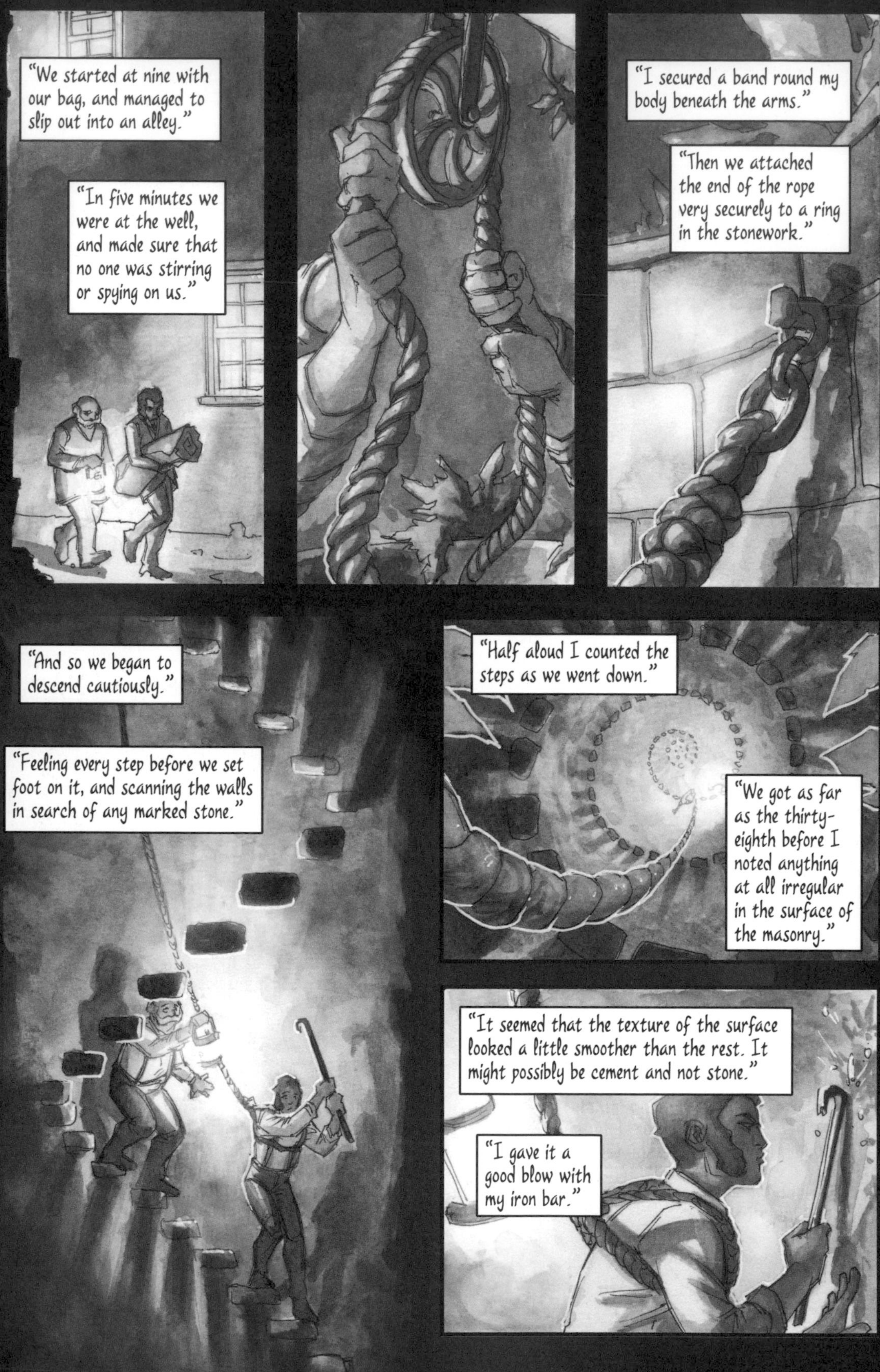

"We started at nine with our bag, and managed to slip out into an alley."

"In five minutes we were at the well, and made sure that no one was stirring or spying on us."

"I secured a band round my body beneath the arms."

"Then we attached the end of the rope very securely to a ring in the stonework."

"And so we began to descend cautiously."

"Feeling every step before we set foot on it, and scanning the walls in search of any marked stone."

"Half aloud I counted the steps as we went down."

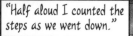

"We got as far as the thirty-eighth before I noted anything at all irregular in the surface of the masonry."

"It seemed that the texture of the surface looked a little smoother than the rest. It might possibly be cement and not stone."

"I gave it a good blow with my iron bar."

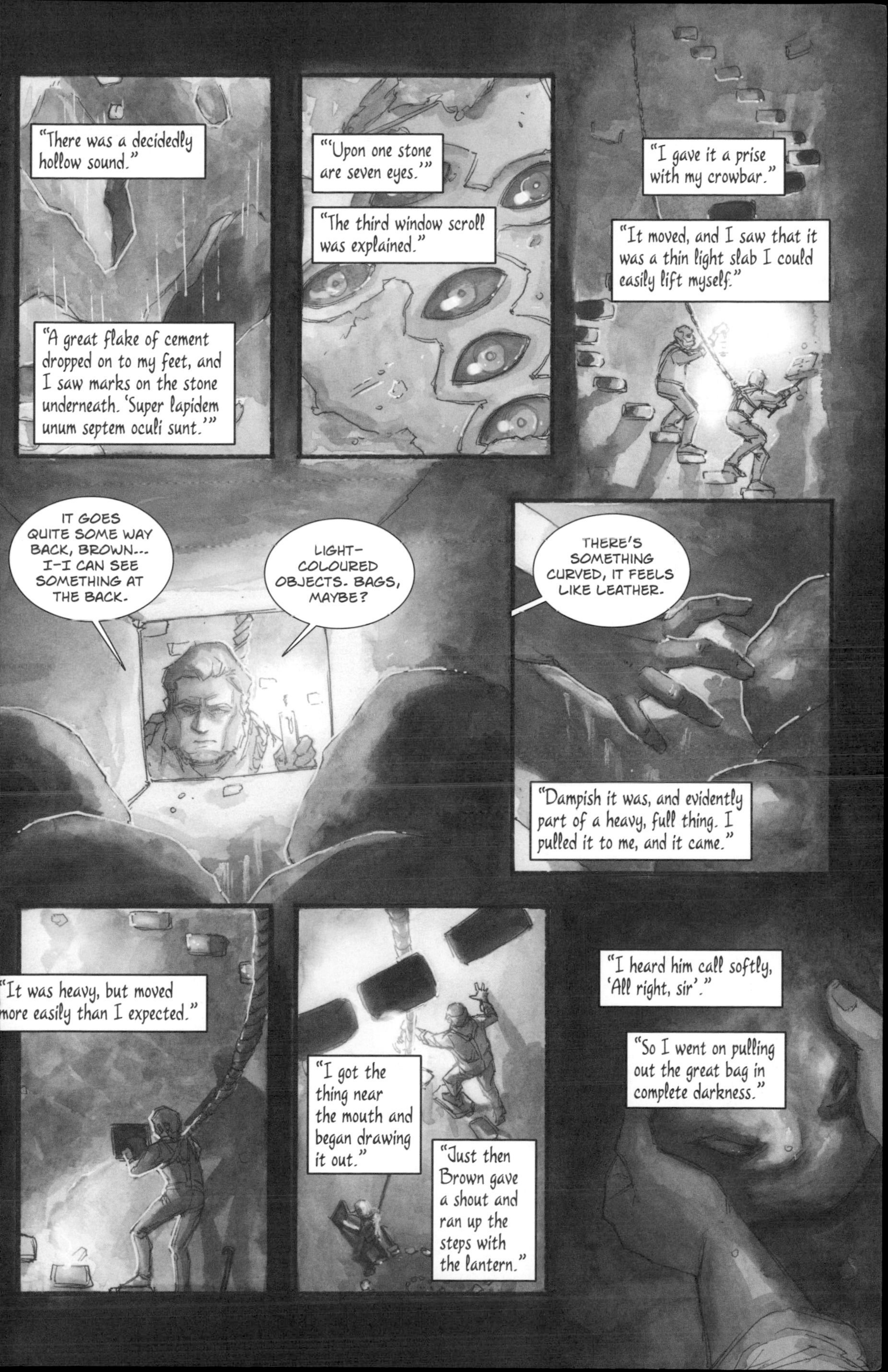
"There was a decidedly hollow sound."
"A great flake of cement dropped on to my feet, and I saw marks on the stone underneath. 'Super lapidem unum septem oculi sunt.'"
"'Upon one stone are seven eyes.'"
"The third window scroll was explained."
"I gave it a prise with my crowbar."
"It moved, and I saw that it was a thin light slab I could easily lift myself."
IT GOES QUITE SOME WAY BACK, BROWN... I-I CAN SEE SOMETHING AT THE BACK.
LIGHT-COLOURED OBJECTS. BAGS, MAYBE?
THERE'S SOMETHING CURVED, IT FEELS LIKE LEATHER.
"Dampish it was, and evidently part of a heavy, full thing. I pulled it to me, and it came."
"It was heavy, but moved more easily than I expected."
"I got the thing near the mouth and began drawing it out."
"Just then Brown gave a shout and ran up the steps with the lantern."
"I heard him call softly, 'All right, sir'."
"So I went on pulling out the great bag in complete darkness."

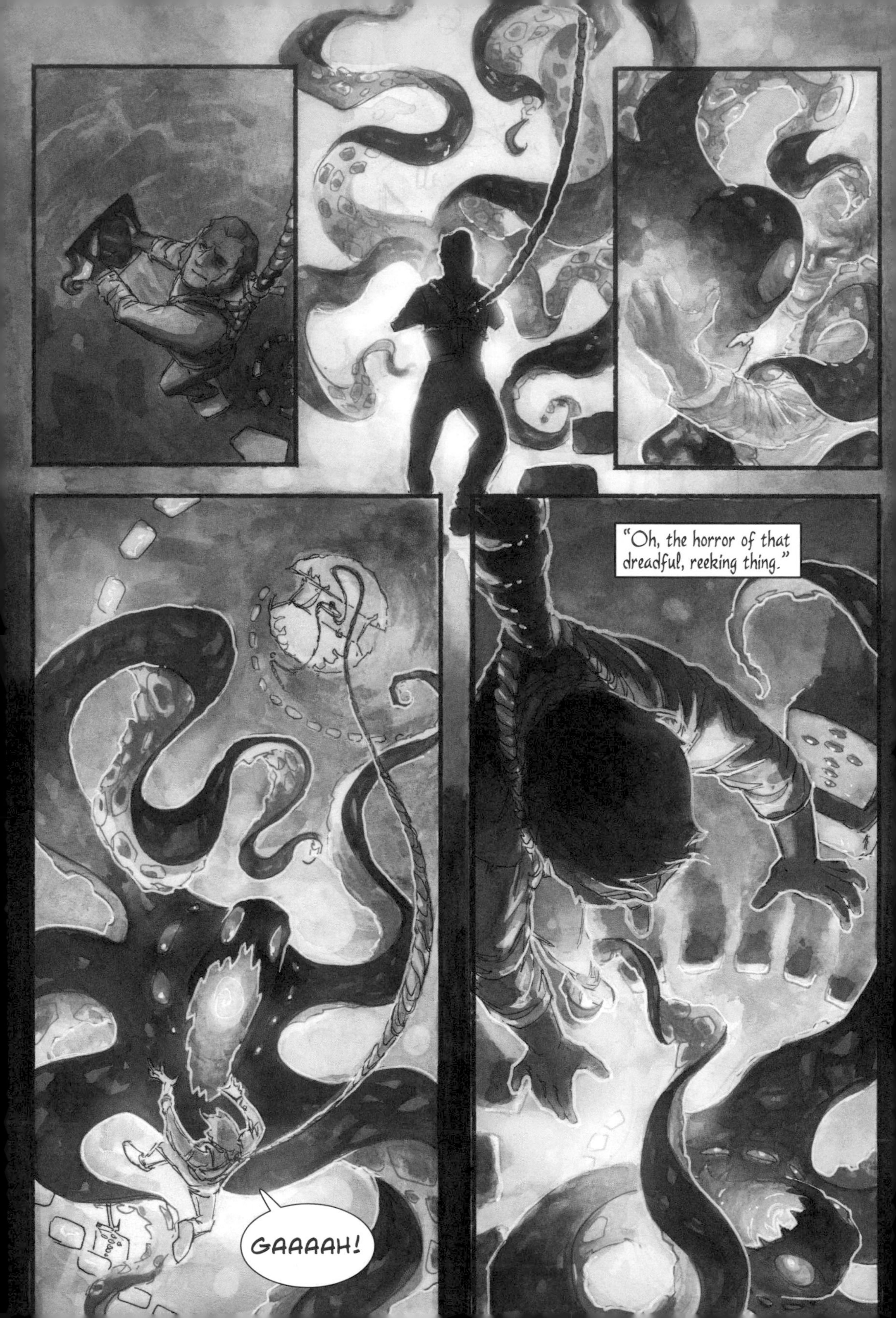
GAAAAH!
"Oh, the horror of that dreadful, reeking thing."

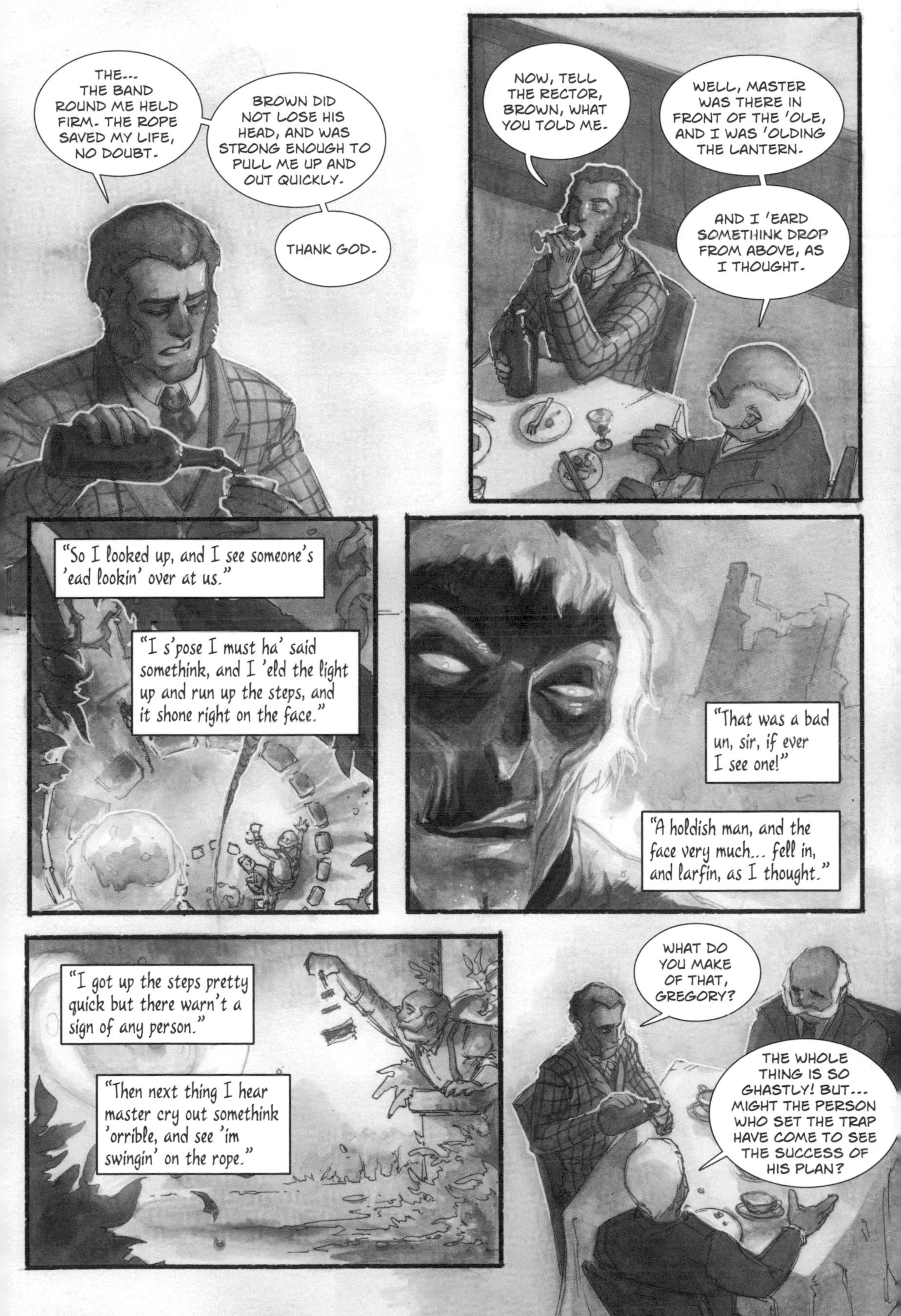
THE--- THE BAND ROUND ME HELD FIRM- THE ROPE SAVED MY LIFE, NO DOUBT-
BROWN DID NOT LOSE HIS HEAD, AND WAS STRONG ENOUGH TO PULL ME UP AND OUT QUICKLY-
THANK GOD-
NOW, TELL THE RECTOR, BROWN, WHAT YOU TOLD ME-
WELL, MASTER WAS THERE IN FRONT OF THE 'OLE, AND I WAS 'OLDING THE LANTERN-
AND I 'EARD SOMETHINK DROP FROM ABOVE, AS I THOUGHT-
"So I looked up, and I see someone's 'ead lookin' over at us."
"I s'pose I must ha' said somethink, and I 'eld the light up and run up the steps, and it shone right on the face."
"That was a bad un, sir, if ever I see one!"
"A holdish man, and the face very much... fell in, and larfin, as I thought."
"I got up the steps pretty quick but there warn't a sign of any person."
"Then next thing I hear master cry out somethink 'orrible, and see 'im swingin' on the rope."
WHAT DO YOU MAKE OF THAT, GREGORY?
THE WHOLE THING IS SO GHASTLY! BUT... MIGHT THE PERSON WHO SET THE TRAP HAVE COME TO SEE THE SUCCESS OF HIS PLAN?

"Just so, Gregory, just so. The Abbot himself!"
"Well, I haven't much more to tell you."
"I spent a miserable night, Brown sitting up with me."
"Next day I was no better."
"Unable to get up, no doctor to be had - I doubt if he could have done much for me, anyway."
"I made Brown write off to you, and spent a second terrible night."
"And, Gregory, of this I am sure, there was someone or something on the watch outside my door the whole night."
"I almost fancy there were two."
"Every rag I had had on me on that first evening I had stripped off and made Brown burn."
"Yet the smell was there, as intense as it had been in the well."
"It came from outside the door."
"But with the dawn, the stench and soft sounds ceased."
"That convinced me that the things were creatures of darkness, and could not stand the daylight."
"So the stone could be replaced safely while the sun shone!"
"The rest you know."

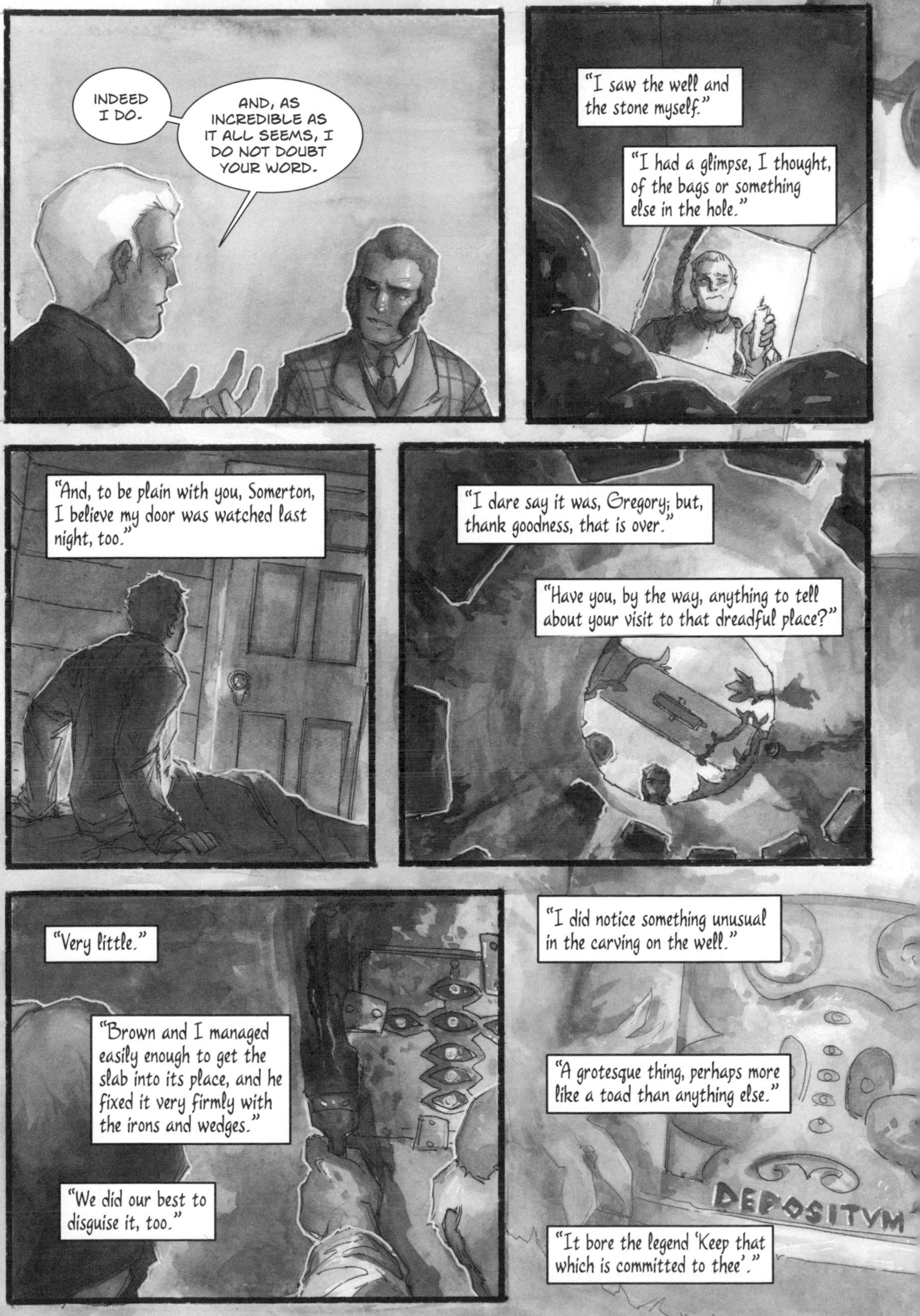

INDEED I DO.
AND, AS INCREDIBLE AS IT ALL SEEMS, I DO NOT DOUBT YOUR WORD.
"I saw the well and the stone myself."
"I had a glimpse, I thought, of the bags or something else in the hole."
"And, to be plain with you, Somerton, I believe my door was watched last night, too."
"I dare say it was, Gregory; but, thank goodness, that is over."
"Have you, by the way, anything to tell about your visit to that dreadful place?"
"Very little."
"Brown and I managed easily enough to get the slab into its place, and he fixed it very firmly with the irons and wedges."
"We did our best to disguise it, too."
"I did notice something unusual in the carving on the well."
"A grotesque thing, perhaps more like a toad than anything else."
DEPOSITVM
"It bore the legend 'Keep that which is committed to thee'."

ADAPTERS

LEAH MOORE AND JOHN REPPION

Husband and wife writing team Leah Moore and John Reppion have been working together since 2003. During their career, the duo have adapted works by Bram Stoker, H.P. Lovecraft and Lewis Carroll into comics, and have written original stories featuring such iconic characters as Sherlock Holmes, Doctor Who and Red Sonja.

ARTISTS

GEORGE KAMBADAIS

George Kambadais is a freelance comic artist whose previous work includes: **Short Order Crooks**, published by 2Headed Press; **Grave Lilies**, published by Z2 comics; **The Vampire Diaries** #4, published by DC; and **The Double Life of Miranda Turner**, published by Image. He lives and works in Greece.

ABIGAIL LARSON

Abigail Larson's dark, macabre work has been shown in galleries in many cities throughout America and Europe, including New York City, Los Angeles, London and Paris. Her illustrations have been featured in various publications, including **Spectrum Fantastic Art**, **Art Fundamentals**, **The Graphic Canon of Children's Literature** and **Digital Artist**, as well as in books from IDW Publishing, Titan Comics, Pelican Books and 3DTotal.

AL DAVISON

Al Davison is a comics creator best known for his graphic autobiography **The Spiral Cage**, IDW's **Doctor Who** (with Tony Lee) and **The Unwritten** (with Mike Carey and Peter Gross). He runs the Astral Gypsy Studio and Comic Shop with his wife Maggie. Al is currently working on a sequel to *The Spiral Cage*, **Muscle Memory**, via Patreon, and has just completed a graphic novel called **Future Echoes** for Liminal Press, in collaboration with his studio partner Yen Quach.

MEGHAN HETRICK

Meghan Hetrick is a Yankee artist currently living in the Deep South of the United States with her partner and a laughable number of pets. When not fending off zombie attacks due to her proximity to the CDC, you can typically find her painting various pieces for clients including Marvel, DC, VERTIGO and Valiant.

ALSO AVAILABLE

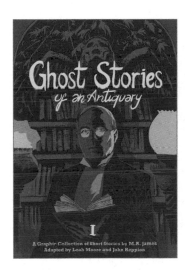

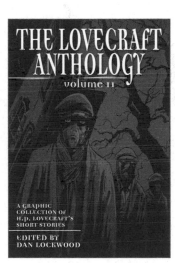

Ghost Stories
of an Antiquary
I
A Graphic Collection of Short Stories by M.R. James
Adapted by Leah Moore and John Reppion

Ghost Stories of an Antiquary, Vol. 1

ISBN: 978-1-910593-18-9
Paperback, 64pp

The Lovecraft Anthology, Vol. 1

ISBN: 978-1-906838-28-7
Paperback, 120pp
US Edition
ISBN: 978-1-906838-53-9

THE LOVECRAFT ANTHOLOGY
volume II
A GRAPHIC COLLECTION OF H.P. LOVECRAFT'S SHORT STORIES
EDITED BY
DAN LOCKWOOD

The Lovecraft Anthology, Vol. 2

ISBN: 978-1-906838-43-0
Paperback, 128pp